CHAZ

REAPERS MC BOOK FOURTEEN

ELIZABETH KNOX

CONTENTS

Playlist — xv
Acknowledgments — xvii
Reapers MC Clubhouse — xxxi

Prologue — 1
Chapter 1 — 9
Chapter 2 — 18
Chapter 3 — 26
Chapter 4 — 35
Chapter 5 — 49
Chapter 6 — 56
Chapter 7 — 62
Chapter 8 — 70
Chapter 9 — 77
Chapter 10 — 83
Chapter 11 — 91
Chapter 12 — 100
Chapter 13 — 108
Chapter 14 — 116
Chapter 15 — 122
Chapter 16 — 129
Chapter 17 — 138
Chapter 18 — 145
Chapter 19 — 155
Chapter 20 — 161
Chapter 21 — 168
Chapter 22 — 177
Chapter 23 — 187
Chapter 24 — 195

Chapter 25	201
Chapter 26	207
Author's Note	217

Chaz

This book is a work of fiction. The names, characters, places, and incidents are all products of the author's imagination and are not to be construed as real. Any resemblances to persons, organizations, events, or locales are entirely coincidental.

Chaz. Copyright © 2020 by Elizabeth Knox. All rights reserved. No part of this book may be used or reproduced in any manner whatsoever without written permission from the author, except in the case of brief quotations used in articles or reviews. For information contact E. Knox.

Cover design: Clarise Tan, CT Cover Creations

Editing: Kim Lubbers, Knox Publishing

Proofreading: Jackie Ziegler, Knox Publishing

Formatting: E.C. Land, Knox Publishing

Photographer: James Critchley, James Critchley Photography

Models: Maria Edelmen & Ash Edelmen

❦ Created with Vellum

Available Now From Elizabeth Knox

Series: Skulls Renegade

Reign

Redemption

Revenge

Relentless

Reckoning

Reclaimed

Reckless

Regret

Reclusive

Retribution

First Generation: A Skulls Renegade MC Boxset

Series: Steele Bros.

Tough as Steele

Stripping a Steele

Protecting a Steele
Steele her Heart
Stolen Hearts: The Complete Steele Bros Boxset

SERIES: REAPERS MC

Scarred
Blackjack
Here Kitty, Kitty
Booger
Widow
Kade
Hawk
Bull
Cobra
Mouser
Dixon
Zane
Amara
Grim
Chaz

SERIES: IRON VEX MC

Enraged

SERIES: ROYAL BASTARDS MC: BALTIMORE/KNIGHTS OF RETRIBUTION MC

Bet on Me
Rely on Me

SERIES: THE CLANS WITH IRIS SWEETWATER

Promised
The Trade
Cherished
Deceit
Love is War
Defiant
Shattered
Ruthless
Covert
Heretic
Venomous
Flawed

SIN CITY FETS WITH LINNY LAWLESS & AUBREE VALENTINE

Switched
Surrender

FULL THROTTLE WITH ERIN TREJO

Against All Odds

Coming in 2020 From
Elizabeth Knox

Demise
(The Clans #13)

Frost
(Reapers MC #15)

Corrupted Love
(Mackenzies #2)

Bossed Up
(Iron Vex MC #2)

Zorro
(Reapers MC #16)

Consumed

(An F/F Driven Novel)

Hate on Me
(Knights of Retribution MC #1)

Inc's Regret
(Satan's Raiders MC #1)

COMING IN 2021 FROM
ELIZABETH KNOX

Filthy Valentine

Ransom
(Love Hack #1)

Twisted Steel: An MC Anthology
(Second Edition)

The Elites: A Dark Secret Society Collection

DO YOU LIKE PARANORMAL ROMANCE?
CHECK OUT ELIZABETH'S ALTERNATE PEN NAME, LIZ KNOX.
AVAILABLE NOW FROM
LIZ KNOX

SERIES: BLOODLINES TRILOGY
Fated by Blood (Free Prequel)

SERIES: NIGHTSHADE
Blood Oath (A Prequel)

SERIES: LONE WOLF MC
Origins (Free Prequel)

COMING IN 2020 FROM
LIZ KNOX
<u>Caym's Fated Mate</u>
Romanticizing the Gods
Bitten Magic
The Elementals

PLAYLIST

Playlist

If I Hated You — FLETCHER
Cold as Stone — Kascade feat. Charlotte Lawrence
Crazy — Kiana Lede
People I Don't Like — UPSAHL
Whore — In This Moment
Unbreakable — New Years Day
Iris — DIAMANTE & Breaking Benjamin
I Should Probably Go To Bed — Dan + Shay
Nobody's Love — Maroon 5
Black Sheep — Kailee Morgue
hate u love u — Olivia O'Brien
Do Me — Kim Petras

Rager Teenager — Troye Sivan
Midnight Sky — Miley Cyrus

ACKNOWLEDGMENTS

My Alpha Team: Courtnay, Michele, Jai, Janet, Taneesha, Kim, Isabelle, Heidi, Cynthia, Jojo, Vikki, and Lisa — Another one for the books, ladies. Thank you for all you do, but most of all for your invaluable feedback. Your input helps me make these the best books they can be, and I love you all.

My Beta Team: Heidi, Rebecca, Danaca, Christy, Heather, Kristine, Stephanie, and Emma— You guys are my last line of defense before my books are published, and I'm super grateful for the work you put in. I appreciate all of your input, whether it's negative or positive. All of your feedback has only helped make the books better before they're on the market and I'm forever grateful.

My Blogger Team— Thank you all for continuing

to support me, regardless of the road I'm going down. I will say this until the day I die, but, without you I don't think I'd be a fraction of where I'm at today. From the bottom of my heart, thank you.

My Editor, Kim and Proofreader, Jackie— And, we've done it again. I've said this numerous times, but we're really the dream team over here. I can't wait for what's coming your way and I hope you're both excited too!

Rae B. Lake, E.C. Land, April Canavan, Jen L. Grey, and Iris Sweetwater— You ladies are my rocks when I need it the most. Thanks for always being here for me through thick and thin. I don't know what I'd do without you.

You're the woman who inspired Chaz's character, with GG's pronunciation of your name. I think I owe his creation to both of you, haha.

You're not only my personal/virtual assistant, but a dear friend and confidante. I'm so thankful for not only the business relationship we have, but the personal one as well. You've been here for me in some of my hardest times and I don't know what I would've done without you.

Thank you for being here, and thank you for being such an integral part of both my professional and personal life.

Love you, girl.

Trigger Warning

This book is intended for mature audiences only. If darker books are not for you, please do not move forward. After re-adjusting my trigger warning system, I will ***not*** be giving any spoilers. Please understand that this is not your run of the mill romance and tough subjects will be spoken about in this storyline. This story could include things like: rape, kidnapping, abuse, domestic violence, drugs, alcohol abuse, and many other potential triggers.

Gone But Never Forgotten

Fist — Former Prez (Deceased)
Cracker – Former VP (Deceased)
Saffron – Fist's woman, Sakura's sister, Sydney's mom. (Deceased)

Billings, Montana Charter

Zane – Prez – Ol' Lady – Octavia
Children: Sydney (adopted), Neo
Blackjack – VP – Ol' Lady – Ashley
Children: Dex (Blackjack's previous relationship), Noelle &
Fist
Bull – Enforcer – Ol' Lady – Alexa
Grim – Sgt. at Arms – Ol' Lady – Natalie
Children: Aggie, Davina, Sorcha (Nat's Kids)
Tex – Full Patch – Ol' Lady – Roxy
Children: Kat
Dracus – Full Patch – Ol' Lady – Roxy
Children: Nova
Bolt – Full Patch – Ol' Lady – Roxy
Children: Jordyn
Zorro – Full Patch
Axel – Full Patch
Hammer – Full Patch

Frost – Prospect
Turmoil – Prospect
Bama – Prospect
Stiletto – Prospect
Siren – Prospect
Doom – Prospect

Las Vegas, Nevada Charter

Damon — Prez — Ol' Lady — Kat
Children: Luna
Dixon – VP – Ol' Lady – Indra
Children: Jalen (Indra's previous relationship) & Khloe
Booger – Enforcer – Ol' Lady – Camila
Children: Ransom
Widow – Sgt. at Arms – Ol' Lady – Tania (A Jackal)
Children: Zoe (Widow's previous relationship) & Talon
Chaz – Full Patch
Cobra – Full Patch – Ol' Lady – Izzy
Hawk – Full Patch – Ol' Lady – Raven
Kade – Full Patch – Ol' Lady – Ivy
Children: Orion & Fate
Mouser – Full Patch – Ol' Lady – Sakura
Ripper – Prospect
Jolt – Prospect
Spark – Prospect

Poison – Prospect
Brick – Prospect
Doc – Prospect
Boulder – Prospect
Rooster – Prospect

Chihuahua, Mexico Charter

Amara – Prez – Ol' Man – Dante

REAPERS MC CLUBHOUSE

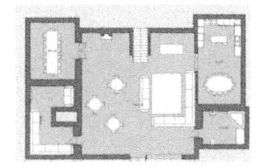

PROLOGUE

I am a black sheep. I refuse to exist when I can live. I refuse to follow when I can lead. I will seek and embrace my true purpose. I will live life on my own terms. I will leave footprints that change the world. And fingerprints that change history.
~ Amanda Louise

Crina
Christmas Day . . .

"WHAT IS WRONG WITH YOU, CRINA?" My eldest half-brother, Mircea, snarls at me from across the table while my mother weeps dramatically. Father simply runs his hand across his face, as he always does when he's displeased with me.

I can't believe he has the audacity to ask me this question. Sorin, my other half-brother, glares at Mircea in disgust. "I'm not a piece of meat to be sold to the highest bidder, unlike what *you* think." I shift my focus to my father, to the man my mother had the stupidity to sleep with— her boss.

"You are a Romanian woman of a high bloodline. Mircea will be inducted into the Clans very shortly and you don't wish to maximize on where our family is headed?" Father speaks, though it's more like a question.

I inhale sharply, trying not to lose it. Whenever I do, it only upsets my mother. And even though she's made poor choices in the past, I do love her. Hell, I even love my brothers. I'd say I love my father, but that would be a stretch. He's only ever viewed me as less than. He's a product of the man who raised him, ensuring him the world would always be a man's world. I bet my dear grandfather never expected women to unite together and get pissed about things like equal pay, being treated fairly, and the plethora of other things we're realizing in this day and age.

"You have never once given a damn about me. I'm sorry, brothers, but you've never given a damn about me in the way you do for Sorin and Mircea. I'm not jealous in the least bit, so don't even attempt to spin it that way."

"Things are changing, Crina." My father tells me with a growl.

"I want no part in the *change* coming to our family. Don't you see?" He only wishes to put a collar around my neck and hand my leash to a prominent Romanian man so I can do something positive in his eyes. So, I won't simply be the product of his affair. I've been the black sheep my entire life and I'll never be anything less than that.

I rise from the plush cushioned dining room chair and stare into his callous eyes. "What is it you're doing, Crina?" He questions, still with the same frustration he's had from a few moments before.

"Weren't you listening? I said I wanted no part of this." I state, pushing the chair under the table.

"Crina, please don't leave . . . your—" my mother begs of me.

"If you leave today, you'd best not ever come back to this table again." My father sneers, balling his fists.

As if it would even matter. "You've only just invited me here." I walk over in the direction of the foyer when the sound of glass breaking against the ground causes me to stop right in my tracks.

"Crina, I mean it. If you walk out of that door, I

will never welcome you back into this family." He goes on with his threats.

Turning around, I look to my dysfunctional family. Mircea seems just as furious as our father does, while Sorin seems plagued by the events that're going down. "I'm not a cow you can sell off to another rancher for him to brand and use me as he wants. Things might've been done that way hundreds of years ago, but now there's something called consent, and I sure as hell don't give it to you."

"You are dead to me." He grumbles.

I can't help but allow what he's said to hit me right in the heart, and the only way I know to hurt him, is to hurt the only person he's ever given a damn about. My mother. "I don't know how you ever fell for such a vile man." It's the last thing I say before I head to the front door. One of my father's household staff members already has my duster coat and purse. As my purse is being given to me, heated footsteps come in heavily behind me.

I slide my hand into my purse to get my keys and just as I'm pulling them out, they're ripped from my hands. My father glares at me with flaring nostrils in what must be his ten-thousand-dollar suit. "This is mine," he dangles my keys in front of my face.

"Oh, really? I thought you gave me the BMW for my birthday."

"I own it. My name is on the car." He completely ignores what I've said.

I see what he's doing here. "Okay." Digging into my purse, I take out my wallet and pull the black cards that're connected to the family accounts, and anything that might have something to do with money he's given me. I throw them all on the floor. "You're trying to intimidate me into doing what you want? Fuck that and fuck you."

Before my very eyes he rips his hand back and starts to bring it toward me when Sorin comes in the middle and shoves him back a few feet. If it weren't for him, our father would've struck me. "I think I've had enough of our typical melodramatic Christmas." He states, glaring in the direction of our father.

Though, Mircea . . . he's probably sitting at the table like the prodigal son he always is.

"C'mon, you need a ride?"

"Yes, please." I state lowly.

"No problem." Sorin replies, wrapping his arm around my waist he walks me out of our father's Las Vegas mansion.

We're to his car and speeding out of the driveway

in no time. "Thank you," I mutter to Sorin, slinking down in the seat beside him.

"You don't need to thank me for anything. Dad's a dick. I think we're all aware of that fact."

"Everyone except Mircea." I point out.

"Yeah, well, Mircea has more on the line than any of us."

"Why do you always make excuses for him?" I question, watching as Sorin's dark chocolate eyes land on mine.

"I'm not excusing his behavior, Crina. I'm only saying things are different for all of us. I'm your *frate*. It's my job to defend you both." He speaks in Romanlish again, which is my personal slang for Romanian-English. If it weren't for Sorin, I wouldn't know a bit of it. Our father never had the patience to explain things to me. "You going to stay with me tonight, considering father has probably disabled your keycodes?"

Shit. I didn't even think of it. "Yeah."

"I have an extra room, so you can stay as long as you need."

I appreciate his offer, but I won't put him out. Sorin is going to die a bachelor and I know it. He has quite the reputation around Las Vegas for throwing the best parties. With his condo overlooking the Strip, he's in the prime location.

"Just give me a couple of days. I'll sort something out. Okay?" I only have one option, or one that is realistic at least.

"What're you going to do, Crina?" Sorin knows me better than anyone else.

"Whatever I need to. I'm not going to live off his money or look to you. I'll sort this out, okay? I know people."

He grips the steering wheel a bit harder. "I don't like the way you said that."

"I'm sure you don't, 'cause it means I'm up to something and you hate it when I'm a mischievous little brat." I smirk, trying to lighten up the situation.

"Fine, whatever, but if you get into trouble or need something . . . promise me you won't be a stubborn, little, shitty, brat. Okay? I'm your big brother, kid. It's my job to protect you."

I nod my head like I'm agreeing, but I won't vocalize it, because I'm an adult. It's my job to take care of myself, and it certainly isn't his, or our father's for that matter.

I got myself into this mess, so I'll get myself out.

CHAPTER ONE

Sometimes you need to give up on people, not because you don't care, but because they don't
~ OurMindfulLife.com

Chaz
Christmas Day

"IT'S SNOWING babies in Montana! Ah!" Raven screams in the middle of the clubhouse, jumping up and down like it's damn near the happiest day of her life. Her two sisters, Danica and Bridget, are right by the tree. Meanwhile, Luna's trying to crawl wherever she can right now. Shit, that lil' one is growing like a weed.

"What're you goin' on about, woman?" Mouser

chuckles from across the way, sitting beside his ol' lady, Sakura.

"Word on the street is, Ashley and Natalie were talking about being pregnant and Grim overheard them both, Blackjack too."

"I must be missing something. Who's Natalie?"

Everyone looks at me like I've damn near lost my mind. "Um, Grim's girl. How did you not know about her?" Raven replies, rolling her eyes.

"He's too busy makin' sure his pickle's wet." Mouser chuckles, careful not to say anything inappropriate in front of her sisters. There's been a couple of times where he's blabbed away without thinking and Hawk has gone off on him.

"Why can't you be more like Dixon? At least he got his life figured out." Raven mutters, always being the one to chastise me for my choices.

"I told you this already, I'm not ready for that shit. Don't know if I ever will."

"Well, I hope you don't die alone." Raven smugly replies, trying to be a bit of a bitch.

Her and I get into it every now and again, but we don't hate each other. We just get into spats. Pretty sure it's because we're both determined individuals. Know what I mean? "Sakura, you on the baby train next?" Raven giggles.

I watch as Sakura's face goes ghost white and she quickly recovers with a soft smile. "Who knows."

Mouser shifts his head to look at her and I notice the way his expression shifts to a somber one. A group of our newest prospects comes rolling in through the front with presents in tow for the kids. Sakura rises from where she's sitting on the couch and heads outside. Mouser starts to rise, but I wave him off, thinking she just might need a friend right about now and not her ol' man.

I follow her out the door and shut it securely behind me. Sakura's already got her hands wrapped around herself, almost in a soothing manner. "Wanna talk about it, or are you gonna tell me to go fuck myself?" I ask.

"You tell me."

"A bit of both. You're usually a dynamite like that." I say, getting a bit closer. "What's goin' on, Sak'?" I call her the nickname I've dubbed her. Since being here, we've become pretty good friends. She confides in me and vice versa.

She leans her head back so her dark hair falls behind her. Rubbing a hand over her lips, I know she's debating on whether or not she's going to say anything. "You know you can trust me." I tell her.

Sakura turns to face me, "I know that, Chaz. I just

don't wanna lose my shit. Okay? 'Cause I've been having a really hard time holding all this in."

Within a moment I feel the heaviness this conversation is bound to bring. "You can talk to me about anything, Sak'. Don't ever forget it."

She gnaws on her bottom lip, still debating.

"It's what Raven said, isn't it?"

"How perceptive." She lets out a sigh, rubbing her hand under her eyes, I realize she's crying.

Fuck me. I'm not the type of man for this shit, dealin' with women all up in their feelings and whatever. I'd do it for Sak' and Cheyenne, though. Without those two by my side I don't know if I ever would've made it through my reconstruction surgeries. They both were there for me, every fuckin' day while I felt like I was losing grip of everything. Shit, the scars on my hands are still clear as day, but they're simply a reminder of everything I pulled myself through.

I walk closer until I'm directly next to her, wrap an arm around her, and pull her against me. I don't know if I've ever loved a woman like this, not in the sexual way, but love her like a sister. I don't have much family, but Sak' and Cheyenne are the closest thing I have.

"I was pregnant last month."

She said *was*.

"We lost it, just like we lost the last one and . . . Chaz . . . I've never felt more helpless. Even with all the problems with my mother, at least I was able to do something then, but this . . . I can't do anything about this. It's all about science and biology and shit, and I know this happens. I know it's normal, but that doesn't mean it makes me feel any better. Even all those years of schooling . . . I was never prepared for how the agony will fester, feeling like it's slowly eating away at your soul." She does pretty good not bursting into tears, but I pull her closer against me and turn so I'm facing the door and she's sobbing into my chest. The harder she cries, the tighter I hold her.

"Let it out, Sak'." I urge her, knowing just how this woman is the rock for so many people here, but she has no one besides Mouser being a rock for her. I can't ever imagine the horrible way she's feeling, but I don't ever wish to. Not again. There's so much about me the club doesn't know. Fuck, I don't even think Roman, who was my old Prez at the Brotherhood MC and also Damon's father, ever knew about my wife and son. At least they both went together. That's the only peace I can find, that they're not alone.

The door opens to the clubhouse and I see Mouser peering out, staring at me holding his girl. Fuck, even he feels helpless as shit. It's written across his face. I mouth 'I got her' to him and he nods, his eyes drifting to the woman he loves more than anything else. 'Go, have fun.' I mouth again as his eyes come back to me. I don't even know why I choose these words, but I'm trying to give him somewhat of a break. He needs to distract himself too, 'cause fuck . . . I know how he feels. He ends up shutting the door, going back into the club. He knows he can trust me.

Tires turning cause me to look up the driveway and I spot Rebel's signature decked out SUV. Rebel is Widow's ex-girlfriend/baby momma. They have a lil' girl named Zoe, who's about eleven now.

Rebel stops the vehicle and parks it, hops out alongside her husband, Nikolai, and he fetches Zoe from the back. "Where's Daddy?" Zoe questions rather loudly.

Sak' tears herself out of my grip, wiping under her eyes and goes around to the other side of the porch. I have no doubt about it that she doesn't want Zoe to see her upset. Kids are perceptive like that. "He's inside munchkin," I smirk, getting a giggle in response from this lil' diva.

The door to the club comes bursting open and Widow comes through, kneeling on the ground so Zoe can come crashing into him like always. "How's my favorite baby girl?!" He chuckles.

"I'm great! Papa Nikolai just got me ice cream. Wanna see?" Zoe asks.

Widow's smile turns into a scowl really quick. "Papa what, honey?" He's trying to be nice, but the anger is evident.

Rebel's smirking from behind Zoe, standing beside her husband, who's also smirking in a devilish manner.

Zoe busts out into a hilarious giggle. "See! I told you both he'd get like this!"

Widow's expression goes to Nikolai and Rebel before it shifts back to his daughter. "Ah, how funny."

"Nikolai didn't think you'd find it funny, but I told him you would!" Zoe smiles, wrapping her arms around her father. She pulls away quickly and goes rushing inside, surely to see what Santa left here for her.

"Thanks for bringing her, I really appreciate it, considering it's not my day and all." Widow says, rising.

Shit, he and Rebel have come a long way. In the beginning, they were some of the two most toxic people I ever saw. I'm just so glad they put their differences aside to give their daughter the best life possible.

"No need for thanks. Just promise me you won't let her eat an entire bag of frosted animal crackers on the way back to the house. Shit, I think I still smell her vomit on the carpet."

"Drama queen," Nikolai mutters underneath his breath, getting a chuckle from Widow.

I'm not trying to eavesdrop, but it's kinda hard to avoid it. Rebel's phone starts to ring in the SUV, so she goes to open the door and taps something inside. Suddenly, a voice comes over her Bluetooth speaker system. "Rebel, I need a favor." A woman's voice says on the other end.

"Sure, babe. What's up?"

"You think Gia would still be game for me becoming a OneEye ambassador? Things have changed, and I . . . I need a place to live and all that."

"Why wouldn't she?" Rebel laughs.

"You know why. Exes. Stuff gets messy sometimes." The woman tells her.

"Pfft, whatever. It's water under the bridge. I'll text her now. Everything okay?"

"Blow up with my family. I'm at Sorin's right now, but . . . I don't wanna put him out for too long. You know? Gia have room at the building?"

"Of course, she does. We have plenty of room." Rebel tells her.

"Chaz," Sakura says, pulling my attention away.

I turn back to face her. "Yeah?"

"Thanks for being my best friend."

"Don't thank me for that shit. Without you, I don't know if I would've made it through." I say, genuinely speaking from the bottom of my heart.

Sak' grabs my hands, tracing my scars and looks directly into my eyes. "You would've, because you're resilient."

CHAPTER TWO

Resilience is not about overcoming, but becoming
~ Sherri Madell

Crina

INHALING DEEPLY THROUGH MY NOSE, I don't know what the fuck I'm doing... or why I'm here. God. This is a mistake. I could've gotten a job anywhere, but instead I chose to call in a favor to my good friend, Rebel. I just had to see if there was an opening here at Crave, LLC... and in doing so I re-opened the can of worms I barely shut in the first place.

It wouldn't be such an issue if my ex-girlfriend, Gia, wasn't one of the owners. I'm sitting in her office wearing a high waisted pencil skirt with a deep sapphire blue blouse. Gold bracelets adorn my wrists and a matching gold chain necklace is around my neck.

Thinking about my outfit I probably chose gold because it's one of Gia's favorite colors and I need this job. I'd rather work for my ex than be a puppet in my father's show, that's for damn sure. I look across her white marble desk where her Apple desktop sits and then past it through her floor to ceiling windows, showing me one of the most beautiful views on the Strip.

Her chair is pleated with gold buttons and it has a deep purple velvet like finish. Everything about this room is simple, yet loud. Just like Gia.

The clicking of heels coming up from the hallway signals to me that someone is coming in this direction. It feels so odd, to be here. I glance over to the makeshift bar Gia had installed when we were together. The matte black bar causes the gold to pop as it's pressed right up against it. She has tequila on the top no doubt, while scotch and other hard liquors sit on the bottom shelf with the glasses.

The door pushes open with a light creak and the clicking of heels grows louder. "I thought this was a joke when Rebel asked if I'd meet with you today." Gia states in her thick accent.

Shutting my eyes for just a moment, I gather myself and turn to face her. As I do, I see she's perfect, just like she always fucking is. The woman embodies power and that's what kills me. Even in her worst moments, she's far better than me. "I need a job, Gia." I push down my ego and tell her what I need, the sole reason I'm here and keep our personal shit buried.

I was the first relationship she had after she broke up with her boyfriend a couple years ago. His family found out what she did for a living, and then they reconciled. Add in his parents figuring out who exactly Gia was, and who her family is and well, they weren't accepting of the criminal affiliations. We sort of fell for each other on a whim, something that shouldn't have happened, but did. It was fast, hot, and we both fell hard.

Unlike Gia, I don't do everything my father asks of me. Ultimately, it caused the two of us to have intense fights, resulting in our demise.

Gia crosses her arms over her chest in her bright cherry jumpsuit and smirks. "This is almost as good as seeing you beg."

I roll my eyes. "If you're not even going to entertain the idea, I'll leave right now. I'm not here to waste time." I growl, rising from the chair I turn my body toward hers and keep the distance between us.

She slides her hands into the pockets of her jumpsuit, smirking like the devil. "What would you suggest you do here, be part of the girlfriend experience, OneEye? We have many different platforms these days. Many different... options for women like you."

Women like me, blah, blah, bullshit. "OneEye would be preferred." I state, trying to keep the emotion in my voice at bay. OneEye is an adult subscription service where women take exposed photos of themselves and get an astronomical amount of money. Essentially, it's not only nudes, but you can get tokens for typical photos as well. Lingerie, dresses, it doesn't matter. The people who pay for this service just want to see you dress up, or dress down. Luckily for them, I love to do both.

"I see," Gia murmurs, keeping her eyes on me.

"I need a place to stay." I state, making sure she understands what I need.

Crave, LLC has always given their girls a safe place to stay. They own the top four floors to this skyscraper. The top floor is the club, and below it is an extension of the club . . . for darker tastes, and if people prefer to dive in the world of BDSM, group sex, or a variety of other options. The floor below that is the apartments for the Crave girls, and the apartments go down to this level, split fifty-fifty with their offices and some business ventures.

"What happened to your apartment?" She questions.

"I don't think that's an appropriate question for a potential employer to be asking a potential employee," I state, wanting to keep this strictly professional.

Gia snickers, "If you wanted a clean slate, baby, you shouldn't have come here. You and I will always be more than . . . *this*. We have too much history."

"Funny you say that now, when you were so ready to throw it out the window for your father." I quip, getting angrier as I think about it. Shit. I didn't want her to see me get emotional.

"I've made mistakes in the past. I won't lie about it. Fuck, I won't even deny it. I made the wrong choice that day and I've regretted it ever since. Look, I don't know what you want from me, Crina. Is it really a job, or is it something else?" Gia asks with wide eyes.

"I only want a job. I can assure you, I don't want whatever it is you think I do." I snip, glaring at her.

She chose her precious family over my love for her. That is something I will never forget.

"Fine. You know that only specific Crave girls live here. Either the girlfriend experience, some of our staff that work at night for the club, or a couple of the girls who work for the offices, doing admin work and whatnot. I have those girls sharing apartments, splitting up rooms."

"Alright."

"So, you want to work for OneEye, fine. But, none of my OneEye girls live here. I know you're aware of that. So, you have a couple of options. You can work at the club tonight and we can see where things go and if you don't like that . . . we can find another fit for you. I'm willing to help you get out of whatever mess you're in, but I'm making a . . . special arrangement for you. Is that understood?"

"Yes. Do you have to clear it with Briar, Diem, Emma, or Kiera?" Briar, Emma, and Diem are typically in the Los Angeles office of Crave, while Kiera is the one who heads up their D.C. operation. Hell, Gia only comes out here every other weekend I believe. Unless she's made the permanent move here to Las Vegas.

"No, they'll stand behind my decision. We're short staffed to begin with."

"Okay. What do you need me to do tonight?" I ask her.

Gia struts directly by me and goes behind her desk,

opens the top drawer and pulls out a series of black lace chokers with different colored pearls dangling from each. "Pick a color."

I stare at the chokers, knowing exactly what she's asking me to do. On paper, my job will be classified to be there as a go-go dancer, a sort of entertainer. However, there are many things that aren't on paper when it comes to Crave, and this is one of them.

Each color signifies something different. "Do you remember what they mean, or should I go through it with you again?" Gia asks.

I stare blankly at the colors. "Of course, I know what they fucking mean. I helped you create them." I snap.

Gia smiles, "Then pick a color, baby."

Each color signifies a person's sexual interests. Black is for the darkest of those who wish to play, meaning you could be into blood type shit, deep double penetration, being flogged and anything sort of degrading. Of course, you're supposed to let your partner know your limits. White means you're into kink, but nothing too crazy. Purple means you're a brat and might be into the daddy/mommy scene. Not age play, but the kink. Red is the signifier for being a pain slut, pink is for those who refer to themselves as a babygirl, but I helped Gia also add furry play into that part. Blue means water, so on and so forth.

Okay, Diem created the idea, but I was the one who helped Gia figure out how to maximize on her idea.

I scan my eyes across the chokers, ultimately picking up what I'm sure Gia knew I would— black.

CHAPTER THREE

Do not give your past the power to define your future
~ Unknown

Chaz

"UNCLE CHAZ, why don't you have a girlfriend yet?" Zoe curiously questions me, furrowing her brows like she doesn't understand the fact not everyone needs to be in a committed relationship.

Widow sits back, staring at me from the other side of the bonfire. I bet he's about to club my head in if I answer her the wrong way or corrupt his precious little angel. "No one can bother putting up with your uncle that long, sweetheart." Cheyenne elbows me, poking fun.

Zoe busts out into the cutest laughter, and right about now is when it hits me. My son would've been maybe a year or so older than her. Shit, how I wish life turned out differently. "Momma, did you hear Cheyenne?!" Zoe asks, looking over to Rebel who's sitting on Nikolai's lap.

If someone would've told me years ago that Nikolai, Rebel, and Widow could be in the same vicinity without tearing each other to shreds, I don't know if I would've believed them. Cheyenne is still new to Zoe, so she hasn't exactly earned the aunt title yet.

"I sure did, and it sounds about right if you ask me. Your uncle Chaz has always been up to trouble," Rebel smirks, joining in on the teasing me bit.

"Y'all make me sound like I'm horrible." I tell the two of them.

"No, not horrible." Cheyenne giggles lightly, sitting beside me on the picnic table. She and I have gotten really fucking close, like *really* close, but not that close. Some days I sit here and wonder what it would be like to have a woman like her in my life, but I typically remind myself that with love comes pain, and I don't think I could survive going through shit again. Not the way I did before.

I pick up the green plastic cup I've been drinking out of the last couple hours and smile at her, catching the way her dark eyes glimmer in the light. She told me when I first met her that she was a lesbian, but part of me thinks she's bisexual and she just told me that so I wouldn't pursue her. Shit, with the way she's looking at me now ... it really makes me wonder.

"Why don't you ask Cheyenne why she doesn't have a girlfriend?" I ask Zoe, figuring Cheyenne can get fucked with a lil' bit here too.

Zoe cranes her neck to the side. "How come!?"

Cheyenne chuckles before she shrugs. "Haven't met the right lady, I guess."

"How did you know you liked girls?" Zoe asks, coming a little closer.

"What do you mean? I've always liked girls." Cheyenne responds.

"You always knew you wanted to kiss them?" Zoe asks.

Cheyenne giggles lightly. "Yeah, in a way, the same way I knew I liked to kiss boys ... I just like kissing girls a little bit more if that makes sense."

Zoe furrows her brows, "I'm confused. You like both boys and girls?"

"I do," Cheyenne nods.

Now I'm lookin' at her like she's a big, fat, liar ... 'cause she fuckin' is.

"There's a word for that. A girl in my class is it.

Clare . . . what's the word for liking both boys and girls?" Zoe mutters to herself.

"A bi-sexual." Cheyenne fills her in.

Zoe nods. "Yeah, my friend Clare, she's a bi-sexual."

"That's nice." Cheyenne smiles, feeling a little odd, I think. She's not the girl's parents and yet she's having a full-on LGBTQ+ conversation with Zoe.

Zoe moves in a little closer to us and whispers. I can barely hear her over the cracking of the fire. "Can I tell you a secret?" She asks.

I nod, and so does Cheyenne. "I've always liked girls, too. I haven't told my momma, or my dad yet, or Nikolai. I'm afraid to tell them . . . but I like girls. They're so pretty, and fun, and I really like them. Boys are gross, and so stupid sometimes."

Cheyenne's smile grows so wide, I doubt I've ever seen her smile like this. "That's okay. You tell your parents and Nikolai when you're ready, okay? There's no rush to do it, just like there's no rush to tell anyone else. And do me a favor, kid, okay?"

"What kinda favor?" Zoe asks, curious as can be yet again.

Cheyenne places both hands on Zoe's shoulders, "Don't you ever let anyone make you feel bad for being true to yourself. Okay?"

"What, like mean to me, for . . . liking girls?" She

still keeps her voice low, like she doesn't want anyone else to hear her.

Cheyenne nods. "Yeah, kinda. People can be really mean, and sometimes they're mean about this. They use it as a way to pick on us, for being lesbians, or bisexual, or whoever people like us are interested in . . . but don't ever feel like you need to conform to societies standards. Alright?"

"Okay . . . I guess." Zoe says, getting a little annoyed with how adult this conversation has shifted. She starts to turn and run off, but Cheyenne takes hold of her hand.

"Oh, and Zoe. Don't worry, your secret is safe with us." Cheyenne tells her, getting a smile from the little girl.

Only, it's not just a smile. Zoe whips back around and wraps her arms around Cheyenne. "Thanks, Aunt Cheyenne, you're the best." She says before she darts back over to where her dad is.

Cheyenne and I both lock eyes on the other and down whatever we have left in our glasses. "You wanna tell me why you always told me you went down a one-way street, Chey'?" I try to keep my tone like usual, but it pisses me off that she never told me this.

"I thought you'd try to fuck our friendship up and try to sleep with me. Shit, all the single guys here tried and you know it. But when I said I was a lesbian, it shot them all down."

I shake my head, aggravated she lied. "Pisses me off, Chey'."

"Look, I'm sorry. In the beginning things weren't easy for me here and you know it." Cheyenne wanted nothing to do with being part of a biker club when she got here. Not in the least bit. Her brother's in one. They're actually allies to us, but we don't really communicate with them as much as we do with other clubs like the Satan's Raiders MC, Skulls Renegade MC, Knights of Retribution MC, or even the Iron Vex MC. It's a weird situation if you ask me and given what she's said about her communication with her brother . . . it's a ticking time bomb.

"Need a refill?" Vivi asks the two of us. I don't communicate with many of the girls from the Bad Bunnies Brothel, but I do get along with this one. She's sweet on the eyes and her personality matches everything else.

"That would be swell," I tell her, handing her my cup. I take Cheyenne's and hand hers over too.

"Tequila, or is it bartender's choice?"

"Anything but the rail Mouser gets," Cheyenne groans. Vivi releases a chuckle and walks off while I recall the last time Cheyenne and Mouser decided to try and one up each other. Both of them lost their stomachs that night.

"I hope you know I'm not just lying about being sorry. I didn't do it to hurt you, but rather to keep my footing and protect myself."

"Look, I know you didn't mean shit by it, but lying is never the way to go. You're not a dumb woman, Chey'." I mutter. Shit, I didn't realize how much her words really hurt me.

Vivi comes strutting back over in her denim short-shorts that her ass is peeking out of, handing us our drinks. "Thanks, Vivi." I say, shifting my eyes right back over to Cheyenne.

She takes a sip and meets my eyes. "Surely you'll cut me some slack."

"Yeah, maybe a little. What makes you think you deserve more than that?"

Her eyes widen and before I realize it, she's thrown her drink in my fucking face. I'm soaked. "Are you kidding me?" I hiss in complete outrage.

"I could say the same damn thing." She shakes her head, furious as can be. "I was by your damn side the entire time you went through those surgeries. Sakura and I, we were there for you, operating on freaking twelve-hour shifts. Who was the one there in the middle of the night when you were waking up from the pain, or the nightmares? Who was the one there when you wanted to give up and end it like Lauren did? I was. I was the one there, touching you, making sure you knew you had fucking support. I lied to you about one small thing and here you are, preaching to me about how I might not deserve your understanding? Fuck you, Chaz." Cheyenne snarls, glaring at me like she never has before.

"Don't say her name," I warn.

No one ever gets to speak about Lauren. Fuck, I don't even speak about her.

"Why? So you can just forget she even existed, or Eli? No. Face your truth like everyone else faces theirs." Cheyenne shakes her head and starts to walk away from me.

I hop off the top of the picnic table and go after her but coming up on my right is Widow. He places a hand on my chest and I flare my nostrils. "Let me go, brother." I tell him.

He shakes his head, "Not happenin', man. You two are both too heated and we have kids here now."

"This is between Chey' and I." I say, staring at her while she walks off.

"Yeah, that's fuckin' obvious. Give her some room to breathe, brother."

I notice Damon walking up from the other side

with Luna in his arms, "Take a walk, Chaz. In the opposite damn direction."

Motherfucker. Shaking my head, I accept defeat and walk off in the opposite direction of Cheyenne. Though, it won't matter. She's gotta come back to the trailer later anyway. She moved out of Sakura's house and has been rooming with me. It'll either be explosive, or cathartic. Guess we'll see.

CHAPTER FOUR

I won't be remembered as a woman who keeps her mouth shut. I'm okay with that
~ OurMindfulLife.Com

Crina

I STARE at myself in the mirror, looking at the platinum blonde wig I'm wearing. It stops just below my ass. It's so platinum the color is almost white. I pick up my matte crimson red lipstick and lean in closer to the mirror, careful as I drag it over my lips to not mess up. Pressing my lips together, I smudge the lipstick and back up to look at myself.

My lips match the red peeking out through the lace number I have on tonight. I have on four-inch heels with black stockings. My panties offer full coverage, continuing the lace and the red rose design. It stops maybe two inches under where my bra does, making me look like a decadent present wrapped securely in a lovely bow.

I place my hands on both ends of my hair and pull about half to the front, giving me a bit of dimension. Lifting my chin up, I stare at the pearl . . . wondering what the fuck I'm doing with my life. It already feels like I've traded one prison for another, even if it was unintentional.

I suck in a breath, throw on my trench coat, and hope Sorin doesn't see me. He went over to my house to fetch some things for me, and luckily he was able to get past the front door by entering our father's birthday as the passcode. Though, the task I have him doing for me is actually the only way to hope we don't cross paths.

I hurry out of the guest bathroom and walk through his condo. My heels click and clack against the marble floors and before I know it, I'm on my way down the elevator. Within a few minutes I'm in the back of an Uber on my way to Crave, LLC.

The driver assumed I was some sort of performer here in Vegas, and I simply nodded and told him that. It's better he doesn't know where I work, or what I do.

I can't believe what I'm about to do tonight. The reality sinks in while I'm in the back of this damn car. I'm about to offer my body up to someone for cold, hard cash. Though, if I'm being honest it's probably enough cash to last me a month . . . if I decide to be a minimalist. I could, and if I have to, I will. It's as simple as that.

I suck in a sharp breath as he pulls in front of the skyscraper. Since I've already paid through the app I head straight inside the building. My phone begins to buzz in my small crossbody purse, so I pull it out and see it's my brother.

From: Sorin

I won't be back until late. Don't wait up.

I spot another notification indicating I've missed another text, so I scroll down and tap away.

From: Mircea

If you want to come back, you still have time. He hasn't casted you out yet, sister.

I'm quick to type a reply to both of my brothers.

To: Sorin

All good. Same here. I should have a place within the next couple days.

To: Mircea

Go fuck yourself, ass kisser.

I slide my phone back into my purse and walk

through the lobby, head toward the elevator, and pull out the keycard that'll grant me access to any of the four floors. Only Crave girls have the keycard allowing access to all four floors, while clients have access to the top two. Fortunately, I was the only one in the elevator on my way up.

I take in a deep breath as the doors open to the club and walk into the thumping music and darkness with only the neon purple and pink lights on display. I strut forward and approach the coat check, giving them my trench. The man hands me a card so I slide it into my purse, determined to keep that on me tonight. Plus, if I'm going to get tipped, I'll need it to stash my cash.

I move further into the club, heading directly over to the bar. Getting through this night isn't going to be possible without some liquid courage. One of the girls comes up behind the bar and walks over to me, "What can I get you, babe?"

"Tequila, on the rocks, please."

"For sure," She says over the music, smiling. After a moment she brings it over and narrows her eyes in on me. "Crina? Is that you?"

I don't know this woman at all, or at least I don't think I do. "Who's asking?"

"It's Bea. I've had a lil' work done, babe." She smirks, pointing to her lips, nose, and tits.

"Holy shit! You look amazing. I had no idea you . . . wow, you look so good." I tell her.

Her smile grows, "Thanks so much. You here for some pleasure?"

I laugh, "No. I work for the company."

Bea blinks a couple times while she processes that. Everyone here knows I dated Gia. For fuck's sake, I was always around. "Gia . . . she let you come . . . work here?"

I nod, "Yep. She's the one who told me to choose one of these." I point to my choker.

Bea presses her lips together. "I smell trouble already. If I remember correctly, she was quite possessive over you."

"Yeah, she was." I agree, though it wasn't in a bad way.

"I should warn you, I'm pretty sure I saw that hottie of a brother you have here." Bea teases, licking her bottom lip.

"Sorin?" I question, suddenly getting nauseous.

"Uh, no, the one with hair."

"Fuck!" Mircea had to be here tonight. Fuck me sideways.

"Do me a favor and flag me down if you see him anywhere close to me. I don't want to get—"

"Oh, honey, he's already in the dungeon. Don't you

worry about that. Last time he was there for about five hours." Bea giggles. Meanwhile, I want to vomit. I physically feel the bile rising in my throat.

"God, please stop while you're ahead. *Please.*" I practically beg her.

"Fine, ruin my fun. Anyway, you're really working tonight . . . on the floor?"

I nod, "Yeah. Gia told me it's what she wanted, so here I am."

"You're right. It is what I wanted. Now come along, baby. I have a client for you." Gia's voice comes out of nowhere, causing a chill to run down my spine.

I turn to face her, seeing her decked out in a deep sapphire blue bodysuit. The lace hugs every curve and crevasse of her body. "What? When did things start working like this?" Never has anyone grabbed clients for the girls. They're always choosing who they spend time with.

"About six months ago we implemented a program called matching. I'm sure you can figure out how it works. Now, come. I don't have time to waste tonight." Gia starts to walk off, and I follow her, but before I do I down the tequila Bea made for me.

Gia leads me downstairs which causes my heart to race a mile a minute, especially since I know my brother is here. Halfway down the stairwell Gia comes to a halt and turns to look back at me. "What's the matter?"

"Mircea is here."

Gia rolls her eyes. "He's too busy balls deep in pussy to pay attention to who's walking by. Come on, unless you want to have a discussion like this in the hallway and have him see you."

As much as I don't want to admit it. She's right. So, I break the distance between us and we head down the rest of the stairs. Gia makes a left toward some of the private rooms and we continue going through the corridor until we're in front of the infamous red room. With a red velvet door, it eludes to what is behind it. Red fabric, red accessories, and red lighting. Of course, there's the occasional black bit.

She swipes her card, opens the door and I follow her in. I walk further into the room to see the red chandelier has actually been replaced with a white one. While there's still bits of red light in the room, it's not nearly as strong as it was a couple years ago.

"Who's the client you matched me with?" I question, hearing the distinct sound of the deadbolt locking. At this point I turn and watch as Gia strips from her blue getup. She's already torn off her top, simply leaving the lace bottoms and heels on.

Her nipples harden in the light as she approaches,

going to the right where a velvet dresser is. She opens the top drawer and tosses me a stack of what must easily be two-thousand dollars. "You said you needed a place to live. This will be the price you pay for it. After today, you don't have to do this again . . . but fuck, Crina, you know better than to dangle a piece of bloody meat in front of a shark. But you did it anyway," Gia smirks, licking her bottom lip as she pulls something else out of the top drawer.

Approaching me, she teases her nipples. I can see the double dildo in her hands, knowing exactly what she wants— *me*. It has one part that she'll slide through the strap on, inserting it inside her where it'll apply pressure to her G-spot, and another part for penetrating the partner. In this case, me.

"Gia, this isn't a good idea."

She cackles, "You're right, it's a great one."

"There's too much between us. This will get messy and we both know it." I try to tell her, thinking about how we ended things. It was horrible. The messiest breakup I've ever been part of.

"Would you be talking to another client this way?" She asks, staring directly into my eyes.

I inhale through my nose and notice the way she watches my chest rise and fall. She grows closer, "As a matter of fact, I'll just check and see if your body's agreeing with this lovely idea of mine." She hooks her fingers underneath my lace panties and pulls them down, revealing my bare pussy. Gia pinches my inner thigh, causing me to open my legs and slips her fingers through my lips.

Her smirk grows and I know there wasn't any hiding it from her.

We might've been good together once, but we won't be anymore. However, she was the best sex I've ever had.

Gia pulls her hand up and shows us both the way her fingers glisten with my essence. She smears her finger against my lips, pushing past my lips so I'm forced to taste my own excitement. "Take off that fucking bra," She hisses, yanking her hand from my mouth.

Gia takes a step back and removes her bottoms, positioning the dildo inside her. I watch as she clicks a button and it begins vibrating. Though, that isn't all. She attaches something to the top and it begins to vibrate and pulsate as well.

I remove my bra slowly and drop it on the floor where she left my panties. Gia comes right up to me, grabs me by the back of my wig and pulls. "You'd better be worth the fucking money I'm throwing your way, Crina."

I slap her across the face before I even realize what I've done. Her cheek flushes with redness from the impact. "Why would you even come this far if you didn't think I'd deliver?" I snarl, shoving her. "Don't even act like I won't give you what you want. I always fucking have, and if I didn't you never would've propositioned me."

Gia licks her bottom lip, "You're right. I wanted another taste. I wanted to watch you quiver like a helpless little slut underneath me, begging me to stop. I didn't know the last time was the last time, and tonight . . . fuck. Tonight, I'm going to make sure you never forget me." She quips, grabbing me by the throat, she bends me over the back of the couch and forces the dildo in my pussy without warning.

It doesn't matter because I'm wet. She's one of those women that has everyone look in her direction. I don't think she's ever met someone who didn't want to fuck her. She pushes my head down into the pillows so my ass is high as she rams the dildo against my G-spot. This might seem insane, but it's like she still knows my body like the back of her hand.

"Actually, I don't fucking like this." Gia says, pulling out of me. She flips me over before she walks away.

She goes over to another dresser, pulls out a big, black cock and smirks as she wiggles it. Every room in here is stocked with fresh toys every night. It's part of the reason they developed an adult toy line, to cut costs and maximize on profits if patrons wanted to take them home.

"This will be perfect." She brings it over to me, grazing it against my lips and I begin to shiver violently as it glides against my clit. "That's what I thought. You've always been such a needy little whore." She laughs as she says the last bit, then pushes the cock inside me. It stretches me wide, burning as she goes further. She goes in and out, pushing and pulsing, bringing her lips down to my clit she sucks while she defiles me.

I close my eyes, loving the way her mouth feels against my lips and the burning sensation shooting through my core. She's always had a knack for being rough with me, and it's one of the things I've missed about being with her. She was gentle, but ever so harsh.

She was exactly what I fucking needed.

An inferno burns within me and I come undone quickly, releasing myself over her. She cackles, loving how I've given in. "I fucking knew you missed me," She mews, flicking her tongue against my clit. "Remember the parties we used to have with my friends, how you'd suck on a clit while you were being fucked in the ass and pussy? God, I fucking miss that. I miss the way our sheets used to smell." Gia removes the cock from my pussy and presses it against my ass, "But more than anything I miss the way you'd beg me to stretch this tight asshole of yours like it was your pussy. As a matter of fact, hold that thought." Gia shoves the cock inside me maybe another inch and I watch as she goes to the entry of the room. She unlocks it, walks outside and within a couple minutes she's back.

Only, she's not alone.

She has a naked blonde with her. "Here," Gia tosses her a pair of panties to hook the dildo in my ass on and the girl comes over. "Baby, this woman here is an extension of my cock. Got it?"

I nod.

"Good." Gia mutters, coming back over to me, she takes the back of my hair yet again and pulls me up. The woman she brought in goes behind me and I feel the dildo shifting inside me as she secures it.

I moan lightly, loving the way it feels. "Come here," Gia instructs, putting me over the arm of the couch. The woman behind me rocks slowly in and out of me while Gia strums my clit like the pick of a guitar before sliding the vibrating dildo back inside me.

I lean my head back, close my eyes and revel in the

euphoric feeling rushing through me. A hand wraps around my throat and I open my eyes, seeing Gia staring me down. Her lips are maybe a millimeter away from mine. She darts her tongue out across my lips and before I know it, I'm crashing my lips against hers. Like two parted bodies of water meeting again for the first time in eons, we crash and combine into one.

Gia fucks me harder, and my ass is being fucked even harder than before. My core flushes with raging heat and I'm so close to release. She brings her other hand up to knead my nipple, teasing, tweaking, and pinching. I thrash as my body begins to give in yet again.

Before I realize what's happening, I feel wetness sliding down my eyes. The pain of getting fucked in my ass with the pleasure of what Gia is bringing my way is too much.

It's causing so much fucking conflict within me, remembering how we broke up, how we were so close and just . . . faded into the background like neither of us ever existed.

Gia tears her lips from mine. "If you're going to cry like a little bitch, then I'm going to give you a reason to after you cum for me. Then I'll make you cum again. Is that understood?"

I nod, not realizing how much I needed to be dominated.

Gia isn't a Mistress, or anything of that sort... but she is a kinky fucking dominator, and that's exactly what I need.

But not after tonight— hopefully I'll find that dominating person I need, but it can't be Gia.

It just fucking can't.

CHAPTER FIVE

Silence the angry man with love. Silence the ill-natured man with kindness. Silence the miser with generosity. Silence the liar with truth.
~ Buddha

Chaz

I WATCH the way the amber liquid in my cup swirls around, floating over the ice, splashing against the sides of the glass. It's my third glass of scotch and I'm still sitting on the dark gray sectional, staring at the front door like a husband who's waiting for his wife to show up.

Glancing over to the oven, I can see from here that

it's a little past one in the morning. Fuck. Where is she?

I run my hand across my forehead in frustration, pissed that I let Damon tell me to take a walk. If I hadn't, she and I would've gotten over this by now. Fuck, we'd both be asleep in our beds, getting some much-needed sleep.

Tires rolling over the gravel driveway indicate someone's driving back, and then I spot headlights in the distance. The lights suddenly stop and I'm on my feet, heading to the door. The second I open it up, I see Camila's shitty little car. She gets out of the driver's side, Cheyenne's in the passenger seat and when the three girls come out of the back, I instantly recognize Cirque, Mirage, and Esme.

"He's already waiting for you," Esme murmurs, probably hoping I wouldn't hear a word of it.

"Fuck," Cheyenne's tone tells me she doesn't want to see me, and I'm not overjoyed to see her either. We have some shit to talk about, and we'd better discuss it. I'm not a fan of liars, and she lied. Not even about something little. It was massive.

If I had known that . . . if I'd known what I learned tonight, things might've . . . maybe they would've turned out differently for us. Fuck, I might've even dated her.

I watch as the bunnies head back to their brothel house, careful to not make any eye contact with me as they scatter off. I'm sure they can feel the tension between Cheyenne and I. "Have a good night," Camila says quickly, rushing over to the trailer she has with Booger.

The second the trailer door slams shut Cheyenne turns to face me. Her black hair cascades in loose waves over her shoulders, and our porch light gives enough illumination to spot the dread in her eyes. She bats her lashes a few times and breathes in deeply before she even takes a step. The sparkle of her nose ring causes me to really take in what she's wearing.

A black thing goes around her breasts, almost looking like a crop top, but it isn't. There aren't any straps on it at all. She has a matching black leather skirt with a zipper going in an asymmetrical way, and to top it all off, she's wearing the sluttiest, velvet red knee-high boots.

"You have fun tonight?" I'm not askin' her to be a dick. I genuinely want to know.

"Cut the bullshit, Charlie." Cheyenne hisses, calling me by my legal name.

She struts up the stairs that lead to our trailer and places her hand on the doorknob. I don't know why, but I grab her forearm. It felt like I needed to, like it would be a way to show her with one touch that I don't want to fight. How I just want to talk.

She doesn't even look at me, her eyes on the brown door in front of her. "*Charlie.*"

Her tone is a warning, a defeated one, but a warning nonetheless.

"I'm sorry I lost my temper with you earlier, okay? It was wrong that I . . . treated you like that."

"I don't understand why you're apologizing." She tells me, pushing the door open she goes inside. I take in a deep breath and follow her in, shutting the door securely behind me.

"Why do you have to second guess my apology? Can't you just accept it like normal women can?"

She whips her head in my direction quicker than she ever has before. "No, because you're not a normal man. You're constantly speaking in fucking riddles, and you know it. Fuck. I know you, Charlie, and I know you have some idea. It's the only reason you're apologizing to me right now, isn't it?" She cocks a brow, crossing her arms while her lips form into a scowl.

I look at her, the way she's dressed fuckin' perfectly. I picture her as the woman who could be on the back of my bike, for good. I tell everyone I'm not the settling down type, but I'd only need the right woman . . . and imagine how I felt when I discovered the right woman might've been here with me all along.

Fuck it.

She has been here all along.

I finish off the rest of my scotch and place the glass on the side table next to the sectional. "It felt like a slap in the face today, Chey'. I thought you were out of my fuckin' league. I thought that you didn't like—"

"Stop." She interrupts me, her eyes going wide. I'm sure she's already caught on with what I'm trying to say.

"Chey', I—"

"No. Shut your mouth. You can't say this to me. Not now."

I narrow my eyes in on her, "What's that supposed to mean?"

Cheyenne sinks back onto the couch, runs her manicured nails through her hair and sighs heavily. "I spoke to Zane this afternoon. Now that you're healed up, he wants me to head to Billings tomorrow."

No.

This has to be a joke.

"You've got to be fuckin' kidding me." I quip.

"I'm not." She confirms.

"I can go with you to Billings." If it means getting what I want, I'll make a sacrifice. I'll go up to Montana with her. It'll be simple, especially if it works out. I'm willing to try for this shit, and I hope she is too.

Cheyenne shakes her head from side to side. "You can't come with me, Charlie."

"The fuck I can't. It's easy, Chey'. I only need Damon to approve it, and he speaks to Zane. Within a few hours I could get the go ahead." I tell her. You'd never know she grew up with an MC by how much she doesn't understand.

"Charlie, trust me . . . you don't want to go with me. Not when, not when . . . things could be changing for you." She said I was the one speaking in riddles, though it looks like she's taken it up now.

"What do you know?"

"I'm not supposed to say anything." She mutters, drifting her eyes down to the floor.

"Chey', please, if you're gonna shoot me down tonight you might as well tell me what I'm missing. I promise I won't say shit to anyone, but do this for me, please."

She looks back up to me and shuts her eyes for a moment. "Charlie, Zane is going to offer you the VP position in Mexico. He asked me what I thought about you being able to handle the pressure, considering I'm your best friend. He wanted to know what I thought, and I told him you would do a great job. He said he was going to offer you the position formally within the next month, after the charter's construction was finished. Amara is still looking for full patches out her way."

Fuck.

I take a seat on the sectional, place my elbows on my knees and rub my hands across my face in disbelief. "You're not fucking with me right now, right? 'Cause that would be a mean joke."

"I wouldn't ever lie to you about something like this." Cheyenne says. I glance her way and see how she's looking at me. She almost seems sad, maybe even defeated in a way.

"I wanted to give this a shot," I mutter, laughing at the end. "'Cause when you . . . said that shit earlier, I saw . . . nevermind."

"Tell me."

"I saw us together. How we could work. We already know so much shit about each other, and Chey' . . ."

"Don't look at me like that, Chaz." Cheyenne shakes her head, signaling for me to stop.

"Too late." I murmur, knowing it's been shot down before we could even give it a go.

CHAPTER SIX

You can't fight demons you enjoy playing with
~ Unknown

Chaz

"You can sit there and have your dreams, hell even fantasies . . . but we can't act on it. Not when I'm leaving for Montana tomorrow and you're leaving for Mexico God knows when." I know she's speaking with the voice of reason, but I barely see any of it right now. Cheyenne is like a bloody steak being dangled in front of a starved wolf.

I rise up from the couch and go over to her, wrap my hand around her neck and bring my lips until they're almost touching hers. Looking down into her dark coffee colored eyes, I spit my words out, praying she'll give in. "Tell me right now you don't want me inside you and I'll walk out that fucking door. But you'd better be damn sure, Chey', 'cause if we cross paths again I'm taking what we both want."

Her eyes dart back and forth and she closes them as she speaks. "I don't want—"

I release her neck and walk toward the door. I open it and turn back to look at her. "Shit, you can't even look at me and say it. Keep lying to yourself, but I meant what I said, Chey'." I leave the trailer I share with her and slam the door shut, shuffle down the stairs and walk toward the club.

Inhaling deeply, I wonder what I just fucking did. I could've yanked that slutty, little skirt off and showed her what she was missing, but I've never been that type of man. I might be the epitome of an alpha, domineering, hell, maybe even an asshole . . . but I want a woman to verbally tell me they want my cock deep inside them.

Cheyenne was doing everything she could to deny it, but I saw through it. I'll play her little game though, even if it felt like my heart was being torn in two. She doesn't have any idea I think I'm in fucking love with her, and I doubt she ever will.

"You alright, Chaz?" Sakura's sitting out on her

front porch, smoking something. She's not the type to ever smoke. As I approach her, the scent of Mary Jane flares in my nostrils. Shit, I might be takin' a puff of what she's got.

Walking toward her, I shrug. "I'll be fine."

She pats the padded chair beside her and I take a seat, grabbing the joint straight from her hand and take a long drag. "Sorry, but I need this." I add.

"Apparently so," She cocks a brow, casting judgement my way. "Want to tell me what's got you so riled up?"

"Not really," I confess.

"You know you don't have a choice, so how about you get down to it." She chuckles lightly, taking the joint back. She takes a drag while I fill her in.

"Cheyenne lied to me about being a lesbian. She's actually bisexual and . . ." I try to find the right words to explain how I feel, but there probably aren't any. I told that woman so much about my life, figuring she was being honest with me about all her shit. Today I found out it wasn't true, about her secret. Hell, I don't know if I should even call it that.

Sakura places her hand over mine and gives it a squeeze. "You don't have to say it. I already know." She offers me a half smile and leans her head against my shoulder.

Sakura and Cheyenne got so close to me while I was recovering, closer than any of the brothers here at the club if you ask me. "I asked her flat out if she wanted me, and she shut her eyes and fuckin' lied." I shake my head, still in disbelief. Would it really be so bad to give into it one night? Especially if we're about to be torn apart. I've always wanted to be in an officer position, but hell if I haven't wanted to find someone to give me a fraction of what Lauren did. For a split second I thought that was Cheyenne.

"Chaz, I think she loves you too. It was kinda obvious in a way, with the way she'd stare at you from across the room. I don't know why she denied you, but there's a reason. I'm sure you know that."

I nod a couple times, knowing the very reason she did. "Yeah, I'm sure there is." I won't tell Sakura what I know, because Cheyenne told me in confidence and I'd never do anything to break that trust.

"Enough about me, how're you doing?" I turn my head to the left and look down at her.

She sucks in a deep breath and pulls her light cardigan closer to her body. "I'm okay."

"Cut the bullshit and be real with me."

Her eyes meet mine. "I'm . . . angry at the world. Furious. Pissed. Unable to understand why this keeps happening to us. The only thing I want is to be a mother, Chaz. I just want to have a growing belly with something Mouser and I made, the purest most beautiful thing our love could produce. I only want that, and it might seem crazy, but . . . I don't understand why it's not working out for us."

I wrap my arm around her and pull Sakura against my side. "Life can be cruel. You know, I don't blame those who want the easy way out. The ones who commit suicide. 'Cause it just means they've gone through shit and they're done with the horrors life can bring us."

"What the hell? When did you get so gruesome? Life isn't about the horrors, it's about the blessings too. I hate losing the babies, I fucking hate it more than I can convey . . . but . . . Chaz, the biggest blessing I ever had was coming across the Reapers path. Without my uncle Eduardo, I would've never met the love of my life, or my best friend." Sakura smiles sweetly at me and I kiss her on the forehead.

"You and Cheyenne are my besties too, if it makes you feel better."

"Cheyenne isn't your best friend, Chaz. She's the woman you love. There's a difference."

"She can't be the woman I love. Don't you see that? She's shot me down." I mutter, taking the joint from Sakura's hand I take another drag and lean my head back, staring at the porch light attracting an abundance of bugs. I watch as they fly toward the warmth and buzz around it, only to get burned alive by the heat once they get inside the bulb.

It's just like life.

The smartest of us thrive, while the rest are torn limb from precious limb.

CHAPTER SEVEN

She has love in her words, pain in her silence
~ Laura Jane

Crina

I ROLL over on the soft bed in my room. My room. It's still a bit hard to believe it. Pulling the faux fur up higher, I wrap myself up looking somewhat like a burrito. Even now I don't know why I did that... why I slept with her.

Do I really want independence so much to dive back into bloody, shark infested waters? Running my hand across my face, I breathe in deeply as my emotions take ahold of me. I loved Gia for a time. Part

CHAZ

of me might even still love her now, but I won't ever be able to go back to what we were. All the actions of last night did was cause me to go back down the emotional rabbit hole I've fought for so long to push back down.

A knock comes to my door and I sit up in bed. "Yeah?" I call out to whoever's on the other side.

"Hey, chica, Gia asked me to tell you to head to her office. She wants to speak to you about a couple things." Bea says, and I'm relieved to know she's in the apartment too. I toss off the blankets and rush over to the door, unlocking it and open it to see such a friendly face.

"I didn't know you lived in this apartment."

"Yeah, me, Fern, and Tildi. Of course, those two are probably sleeping soundly like the hibernating bears they are." Bea giggles, tossing her fire engine red hair over her shoulder. I pay close attention to her features and see how her lips are a little fuller, and her nose is a bit smaller. There's no longer that ridge in the middle of it.

"Okay, I'm sure I'll meet them later when they're awake. But, mmm, I hope you don't take this the wrong way. What're you doing here, in the apartment? I thought you were just a bartender."

Bea's smile drops immediately. "We all have our

own reasons for doing what we do. I won't ask about yours, and you won't ask about mine, alright?"

"Shit. I'm sorry, I just. I was only curious what you're doing for the company." I try to cover up that I was fishing for information, but she knows better.

"I work the high-profile parties, you know, for the obnoxious rich assholes like your brothers." The way Bea speaks makes me feel like she's trying to be rude.

I take the hint she's throwing my way and nod, "Okay, I won't dig. Sorry. Is Gia already in her office?"

"Yep, so you'd better get there quickly before she loses it." Bea says, turning on her heel as she walks off and heads up the stairwell.

I shut the door and change clothes in record time. Thankfully, the girl who was in this room before me must've left some things. Otherwise, I'd be going to Gia's office in a trench coat and I don't want her getting any ideas.

It takes me about ten minutes to get to Gia's office. I push the door open and find her behind her desk, staring down at her laptop with her blue screen filtering glasses on. "It's about time you showed up. I have a job for you." Gia quips.

I continue on forward and take a seat in the black and gold chair across from her desk. A crashing sound from behind me causes me to jump out of my seat. I turn back to find another woman in the office with us.

"Sorry, Gia." The woman tells her.

Gia waves it off, "It's not a problem. I hated that mug anyway." I get a good look at the shattered ceramic on the floor, pretty positive it's the red mug I got for her in Mexico when we were together. God. What a bitch.

"Vic, this is Crina, the new hire." I don't know this woman Gia's introducing me to, but I smile off in her direction. "Crina, this is Vic, short for Victoria. She is one of two women who run an imprint for our company called the Cravings Collection. Vic, come on over." Imprint? I've never heard that term before.

"What's an imprint?" I ask, hoping I don't sound dumb.

Victoria walks over and chuckles. Her heels click against the floor and she twirls a finger in her long, wavy black hair. It stops just above her ass, making her look like one of the women who're casted in those shampoo commercials. "Essentially, it's a subdivision of a publishing company. Gia purchased the company I worked for early last year, and asked me, along with my best friend to co-head the imprint. This imprint focuses on dark romance."

Publishing.

Like books?

What in the world did Gia sign me up for?

"Gia informed me you have a great head on your shoulders. Not only that, but you also have a bachelor's degree in English?"

I nod, "Yes, that would be correct. I graduated early this year."

"Amazing, and how old are you?"

"Twenty-one. I graduated early since a bit of my distractions had . . . freed up some time." I glance over to Gia, hoping she realizes I'm taking a dig at the relationship we had. If she wants to be a bitch, I'll top her.

"Perfect. I was telling Gia the other day we needed a new author on our staff. It's amazing timing that you came into the picture when you did. I already have an assignment for you, if you're ready for it."

I nod, playing along. "Sure. What're you looking for?"

"Motorcycle club romance is taking off, and I want the imprint to be one of the founding fathers of this niche. The only way we can do that is if we have multiple people chasing this. So, I want you to develop a five-book motorcycle club romance series. I expect the first draft in my email in two months. Will that be a problem?"

"No, of course not. Do you have any requirements before I get started?"

"Specify if you're going to touch base on any tough subjects. They're called triggers in the book industry. So, if you were writing about assault, rape, etcetera I'd need to know. I also want the manuscript written in first person, present tense." Victoria comes over to me and hands me her card. "I look forward to doing business with you. There should be a laptop delivered to your apartment later today."

Before I can turn around to ask another question Victoria is already in the hallway, walking away from Gia's office.

"What is this?" I ask Gia, meaning whatever she signed me up for.

"I figured you'd rather do an actual job versus me plowing into your wet cunt every week as payment. You never liked the idea of being a whore anyway, so, as long as you write for Victoria, you have an apartment. Catch my drift?"

"Yeah, I get what you're saying." What a fucking bitch. It's no wonder we broke up.

"Unless you'd prefer to be my own personal sex toy. You can always change your mind." Gia snickers, licking her bottom lip. She pulls her shirt down just a tad so I get an even better look at her bountiful breasts.

"No, I'll write porn. Am I all set up for OneEye?"

"You should be. On your way out you can ask technical support."

"Perfect. Do you need anything else from me?" I ask, thinking I should've worded it a bit differently.

"No, you're free to leave. If there's something needed, my assistant will reach out to you."

I take that as my silent innuendo to get out of her office, so I open the door and walk down the hallway. Just as I do, my phone starts to buzz, so I pull it out and answer. "Hello?"

"Hey, Crina, if you're free later today do you want to grab lunch or dinner?" Rebel asks.

Rebel, the one woman who could be my saving grace.

"Yes, that would be perfect. I . . . I actually need your help if you're willing."

"Sure. What's up, girl?"

"Isn't your baby daddy in that motorcycle gang?"

"Widow. Yep. Why're you asking?"

"Gia has me working for Vic and my task is to write motorcycle romance. I know nothing about it, so I was hoping you could introduce me to some of them and maybe I could interview, or . . . I don't know. I don't know where to even start with this."

"Don't you worry your pretty little head. Can you be ready in three hours? I'll take you over and introduce you to some of the crew. And heads up, dress like the hottie you are. Some of the single guys might give you more attention if you dress like a hussy." Rebel causes me to laugh, but I have no problem agreeing to it.

"Awesome. I'm at the Crave apartments. I'm rooming with Bea, Tildi, and Fern."

"Oh, the posh apartment. What did you do to get into that one? Damn."

"You *don't* want to know." I chuckle.

"Okay, fine. I'll see you in a while."

"Bye, see ya." Rebel ends the call and I slide my cell back into my pocket while I make my way over to technical support. Hopefully I can get some content up before my field trip to see the biker gang.

CHAPTER EIGHT

"And you were just like the moon, so lonely, so full of imperfections. But just like the moon, you shine in times of darkness."
~ Quotes 'Nd Notes

Crina

When she said we'd meet up, I didn't anticipate she'd have an outfit for me to change into. Or that we'd be going in her SUV over to the club, which is apparently what bikers call their place, a clubhouse.

"Are you gonna tell me what actually went down, or do I need to dig for it?" Rebel asks from the driver's seat.

I cock a brow, knowing what she's getting at

immediately. "Why do you think something happened in the first place?"

"Crina, you're working for your ex-girlfriend. I know for a fact something happened, now, are you gonna spill it or not?"

"It's not like I have much of a choice since you're nosey as hell." I retort, rolling my eyes.

"Perfect, so you said you had a family blow up. Was it your mom, or your dad this time?"

"You mean my father. Yeah, it was him. It's always him." Rebel doesn't know how my family's in deep with the Romanian mafia, but I'm doing my best to keep that fact from her. It's not something she needs to know and I don't want any harm coming to her. You see, my father is very old fashioned. If someone outside of the family were to ever find out what he does, he'd kill them before they could say a word.

"Okay, so what did the old geezer do this time?" Rebel questions as she makes a right onto an old back road.

"He wanted me to marry one of his business associates' sons, tossing me off to the side. And I know what you're going to say, something about this day and age and women coming so far. But remember, he's an old-fashioned Romanian man. He still believes in finding a good husband for his daughter, like it even matters." Now I'm the one rolling my eyes. Even talking about what he wanted to do makes me angrier than I can even comprehend. He never took any interest in me before, and now he wants to be the person to choose whoever I marry? No. Hell fucking no.

"You know, I'm lucky when I think about it in the long run. My daddy never wanted to stick around long enough for me to pull that shit. But, it all turned out better in the end." Rebel tries to find the humor in her own pain, but I've been the one up with her late at night while she's cried over a bottle of wine about her deadbeat father.

If you ask me, I think my life would be much better without him. Hell, better for not only me, but my mom too. She's brainwashed by him. I'll never understand why she ever fell in love with him. I don't see one good quality, not one.

"Yeah, you probably are." I comment back, smirking.

It's one of the things I've always loved about Rebel. She's real. No matter what situation I've ever been in, I can talk to her about it plain as day and she'll find some reason to make me laugh or forget about the problem in the first place.

"Alright, we're pulling up to it now." Rebel says,

causing me to look directly in front of us. I see a series of buildings and trailers. A few of each, leading me to believe this biker club must be pretty substantial. "I'm going to introduce you to Widow. He's really good friends with the Prez here, so I'm sure we can work something out for you."

"Prez?" It's going to take me a while to learn this lingo.

"Yeah, Prez, it's short for President. They also have a VP which is obviously short for Vice President. Enforcer, Sergeant at Arms, Road Captain and Prospects. I think that's all of them, but you can ask the guys."

"You're acting like it's set in stone." I mutter, furrowing my brows. I know she's well acquainted with this club, but I highly doubt they're going to take kindly to some random woman hanging around, asking questions and putting it into a book.

Rebel turns her head to glance at me while she puts the SUV into park. "Crina, when have you ever doubted my abilities to make shit happen? Ease up, girlie. I got this."

"Fine, I'll let you do your thing." I respond, laughing. She's always been the type of woman who sets her eyes on something and gets it. Essentially, she's the type of woman I'm glad to have in my corner.

I open the door and hop out of her SUV while Rebel does the same. I'm in an old KISS t-shirt with denim shorts and sandals. Though, the KISS shirt is shredded which gives a decent look at some side boob.

The door to the building we parked in front of comes open and I see the man I've spotted in pictures with Zoe. One glance at him and you can tell he's Zoe's father, especially when I get a good look at his eyes. They're both the same shade of Caribbean blue.

"Rebel, I was surprised when you called and it wasn't about Zoe." He says.

"Yeah, well, I have a friend who asked for some help and I know you guys can offer some. Widow, this is Crina. Crina, this is Widow." Rebel introduces the two of us and I extend a hand, as does he.

"It's nice to meet you," I say.

"Likewise." He comments. "Now, how exactly am I supposed to help your friend here?"

"Crina works for the publishing company Crave, LLC bought. She's specifically working in the romance imprint, which leads me to why she needs your help. She's been told to write biker romance because it's the next big fad, and she obviously knows nothing about bikers, so, I thought she could shadow you guys or something? Spend some time here and interview you guys? See how you run the club and all that."

Everything seems to be going fine until Rebel gets to the last part, and that's when Widow's face shifts to something less than pleased. "You know I'd go to bat for you for a lot, but I don't know about this. It seems risky, especially with an outsider coming in and wanting to see how we run the club. It's weird . . . and risky. You know we've had enough people causing issues who were in the club. We don't need more."

"Why don't you go and ask Damon? I'm sure he wouldn't mind helping one of my friends out." Rebel states, popping her hip out as she places a hand on it.

Oh boy. Here we go into super, sassy waters.

"You really gonna pull that card, Rebel?" Widow seems less than pleased.

"You're damn straight. She's my friend. Crina isn't a bad person and I'm trying to help ensure she keeps this job." Rebel grits to her ex.

"Look, I won't be any trouble. I promise. I just need some idea of what to write. She isn't lying. I have no clue about this lifestyle and if I don't get something to my boss in two months I'm fucked. I'll be homeless." I speak for myself and luckily Widow pays attention. "Please, I don't want to fuck this up." I pull out my pouty eyes and hope it'll work on this guy. Though, he looks like he snaps women like me in half for a living.

I watch as he runs his hand across his jaw and curses under his breath, "Fuck. Fine. I'll see what I can do. Come on inside and make yourselves comfortable in the meantime."

CHAPTER NINE

I didn't lose you. You lost me. You'll search for me inside of everyone you're with and I won't be found.
~ R.H. Sin

Chaz

WIDOW's just come into the club with Rebel and some other woman, immediately heading back to Damon's office. Meanwhile, I'm sitting here beside Sakura, both having a glass of iced tea she made. Not the sweet shit, but the green tea. I'm kinda a snob these days when it comes to tea and it's all because of her. She makes the best. It's not overly sweet, but it's not bitter as fuck either.

"Do you know who just came in with Rebel?" Sakura asks, with a sly smirk.

I shrug my shoulders, "Not sure. I haven't seen her before."

"You're shitting me, right?" Sakura giggles lightly.

"Huh?"

"For the first time ever, I know someone and you don't. It feels kinda good. I haven't formally been introduced to her yet, but I've seen Rebel around town with her on occasion." She smirks and I throw my arm around her, half tempted to give her a wet willy. And yes, I'm talking about the stuff we all did as kids.

I've been here for a few years now, but Sakura's been here for a couple. I think it's pure luck she even became part of the club. Her godfather had some issues with her parents and while I can't remember all of it, I do remember the club was tasked with keeping her safe for a while. That's how she and Mouser fell hard. He was the one who was supposed to be with her twenty-four-seven. Only, everyone could figure out really quick what those two were doing.

We didn't have a doctor or any sort of medical professional until she came along. Now we do and we're damn lucky. Hell, she helped stitch up Zoe last summer when she split her knee open after a rollerblading accident and that's only one of the times she's helped the club.

"Guys, Damon wants us all in church." Widow speaks up the second he comes back into view. Rebel and her friend go over to one of the other sofas and have a seat. My gut is telling me this has something to do with these two.

I pull my arm from around Sakura and head off to where we hold church, filing in with the rest of my brothers. Damon is already at the head of the table, and for the first time ever I think we've all made a record in getting here so quickly. Sometimes it can take up to thirty minutes for all the brothers to be here. "Everything alright?" I question while I take my seat and Booger shuts the door to the room so no one can hear us.

For a split second I wonder if Damon is going to bring up the position in Mexico, announcing it in front of the rest of the club. "Yeah, everything is solid with the club, but we have something else to talk about. It might seem miniscule to some, but this will affect all of you if we move forward." Damon states, making sure to meet every brother's eyes at least once.

"I still can't believe we're seriously holding church over this." Widow shakes his head, obviously displeased. It further confirms my assumptions. This is because of the girl Rebel brought into the clubhouse.

"Well, get the fuck over it. I said we're having church, so we're having fucking church." Damon snaps in his direction, getting a chuckle from Cobra and myself.

Damon rolls his eyes at our immaturity before continuing to address the room. "I'm not sure if you saw Rebel's friend here. Her name is Crina and she works for the same company Rebel does. However, I've been told Crave, LLC now has a publishing company under their massive umbrella."

"How does a publishing company have anything to do with us?" Mouser asks.

"If you'd shut your trap long enough for me to answer, I'd finish telling you." Well, Damon must've woken up on the wrong side of the bed. He seems really cranky today. "Crina has been told she needs to write a book about bikers and have it to her boss in two months. She doesn't know anything about us, or what we do, so Rebel wanted to bring her here and see if we'd be willing to help her fill in some blanks."

"Uh . . . like a non-fiction book, or fiction?" Booger questions, drawing his brows together.

Damon immediately looks over to Widow. "How

the hell am I supposed to know that shit? I don't even know the difference."

"Non-fiction is factual, fiction is like Harry Potter and stuff like that." I tell the room.

Damon narrows his eyes in on me, "Who all here is open to helping this lady out with her job? I've been told she'll be homeless if we don't help her."

"See if we can get some extra protection for the club, but I don't see why it'd be a bad idea." Booger is the first to speak.

"I mean, keeping a woman off the streets is important in my eyes so." Mouser adds.

"Do whatever the hell you want. It's not like my opinion matters." Widow says.

"Stop being such a fuckin' drama queen." Damon snaps at Widow.

"I don't care if she sticks around. She's a nice lady. Raven and I met her once before." Hawk mutters.

He goes down the line and sure enough, more of the brothers are in favor of helping her, instead of opposed to the general idea.

"Great. Chaz, since you're the resident smartass you can take lead on this. Anything Crina needs, she'll come to you." Damon smirks, sending a silent signal my way.

"Whoa. Me? What the fuck did I do?"

"You haven't done a damn thing, but you're one of the only men with enough experience who isn't locked down with an ol' lady. No way in hell am I gonna pair her up with someone who's in a relationship. I haven't made it this far by being an idiot. Now, get your ass out there and introduce yourself to that nice lady." Damon says, slamming the gavel down.

"Are we gonna place bets on how long it takes for Chaz to fuck her?" Dixon snickers, getting everyone else in the room to do the same.

"Fuck you," I snap, rising from my seat I head to the door.

"I'd give it a week." Cobra adds as I open the door and walk through.

Fuck. What does it even matter? Damon's right. It's not like I'm locked down in a relationship. I was probably the only feasible option without sticking her with some prospect who doesn't know jack shit about the club yet.

CHAPTER TEN

"Normal is an illusion. What is normal for the spider is chaos for the fly."
~ Charles Addams

Crina

I BREATHE IN and out slowly, wanting to tap the bottom of my foot out of nervousness. It's ironic how my father deals with dangerous men, and yet I'm in a biker club, feeling more fear then I ever have while meeting my father's associates. How odd indeed.

"Relax, Crina. I don't know why you're so nervous." Rebel huffs in annoyance.

"I'm not nervous," I tell her, but she knows me well enough to know when I'm pulling a fast one. Fuck, when I think about it, I've been nervous for eons. Whether if it's to deal with my dysfunctional family, working for the woman I thought I was going to marry, or sitting here on this couch.

"Yeah, okay. I can see through your bullshit, Crina, and you know it." I turn to look at Rebel and she's pushing her mouth off to the side. I know she doesn't want me to feel scared about being here, but maybe it isn't even about being here at all.

"I don't want to fail at this and end up needing my father to come save me." I admit. It angers me so much how he'd only speak to me when it was convenient for him. As a young girl, I never understood the way he was so wishy washy with me . . . but after a while I began to watch it as it unfolded, slowly getting worse. I was like any girl at that age, only wanting to be loved by the man who was supposed to love her the most. To know he only cared about me when it came to his work, or status . . . well, it crippled me.

"You won't. You might hate the fact his blood runs through your veins, but if there's anything I know about your family, it's how no one fails at anything. You're the cream of the crop when it comes to stubbornness and being bull-headed, and that my friend will get you exactly where you want to be. Plus, if you honestly think you're going to fail at this I'm going to wonder if you're the one who actually has a bachelor's in English." Rebel giggles lightly at the end, causing a smile to pull at my lips.

"Thanks. I sure needed that." I nudge her side, and Rebel smiles even bigger.

"It's no problem at all. I'm glad I could've helped you."

"Yeah . . . is it weird being here, when, *she* was here?" I've changed subjects on Rebel, needing for us to not talk about me for a bit.

Rebel was pregnant with Zoe when she moved down here to Las Vegas. I don't know all the details, but I do know enough. Essentially, she caught her best friend and boyfriend in bed together so she ran. A few years later their lives all came crashing together again and Rebel had to learn how to co-parent with Widow. I think the other girl's name was Amara, and Rebel told me how she apologized . . . but I think that was a wound that cut so deep that Rebel will never really heal from it. If the roles were reversed, I'd be super fucked up too.

Rebel shakes her head, causing her bright magenta hair to fall forward. "No, but I thought it would be odd at first. I only really started coming around when she was missing . . . which sounds awful, but, I couldn't be around the club if she was here. Seeing her face would be too much. And I know how that sounds, but at the end of the day, I loved her like she was my sister. I know we're all human and people make mistakes, but damn . . . my heart was torn out of my chest. Then when she went missing . . . I lost it. I never told anyone that, but Nikolai had to keep me together. Amara had hurt me so badly one would think I could never give a damn about her ever again, but I loved her, Crina. It . . . it was horrible. It also made me realize I'd forgiven her long ago."

I nod, acting like I can somewhat understand what she's saying . . . but I know there won't be any way for me to comprehend it. Though, I never want to feel the amount of pain either of those women had been through. All Rebel told me was that Amara was found after being held captive for over a year. Now, that is scary stuff. My father had always told me how daughters of the mafia were some of the most sought after by traffickers. It's one of the only things I think he ever did for me, helping me get self-defense classes and teaching me how to shoot a gun. That's the closest I'll ever get to crime in the mafia world.

The sound of men's joint laughter causes both Rebel and I to turn our heads in the direction the men had gone a short time ago. I spot a man walking out. He's wearing one of those leather vests with patches sewn on it, has on dark wash jeans and offsets the entire look with dark combat boots.

"Chaz, everything okay?" Rebel asks.

He nods but doesn't seem amused in the least bit. "Yeah, Damon's asked me to give your girl here some pointers on the MC life."

The way I'm positioned I can see the crazy amount of shock plastered across Rebel's face. "Oh, really? I thought he'd have Ripper with her."

Chaz cocks a brow. "The only thing she'd learn is what it's like being in Rip's bed."

"Um, excuse me. I'm not that easy." I defend my honor, or at least try to. Let's be real. I doubt I even have much honor left these days.

His eyes shift to my body and I take note at the way he rakes up and down like I'm a fresh cooked steak. Hell, he's probably salivating. "You could've fooled me. You do work for Crave after all, right? I mean, isn't their entire embodiment being sluts?"

"Chaz!" Rebel snaps at her friend while I narrow my eyes in on this asshole.

"You know what, I think I'll just figure this out somewhere else. Sure, I wanted to do some research . . . but no way in hell am I going to sit here and be spoken to like this." I stand and walk over to the front door of the club, pull it open and go outside.

Man. I've been spoken to crassly before, but never anything like that. The screech of the door behind me causes me to turn and I see Rebel walking out, throwing her hands up in the air in disbelief. "I've never heard him talk to someone like that, ever." Rebel mutters.

"Everything okay?" A woman's voice questions.

She's sitting on a picnic table on the left side of their porch. Rebel nods, "Yeah. Crina, this is Sakura, she's the nurse practitioner for the club. Sakura, this is Crina. She's one of my old friends, and she works with me at Crave now."

"Oh, nice to meet you. A friend of Rebel's is always a friend of the clubs."

"Right back at you. So, you said that guy isn't normally like that?" I ask, speaking to both of them.

Sakura looks curious, though doesn't ask any questions. Instead, Rebel speaks up. "Chaz was being an asshole. Damon must've asked him to help Crina, and instead of being a sweetie like he normally is, he was a dickwad."

Sakura's expression falters. Obviously, she knows something we don't. "Cheyenne left for Montana this morning. I'm sorry guys, he's having a rough day. Give him a bit and I'm sure he'll be right as rain."

"Who's Cheyenne?" I ask.

"Chaz is besties with Sakura here and Cheyenne. Zane is the national charter Prez and wanted Cheyenne to come up to Billings to be their appointed medic in case something shitty went down." Rebel fills me in.

"Uh, how do you know all that?" Sakura questions her with a laugh.

"Widow."

"Didn't realize you two spoke like that." Sakura mumbles.

"Yeah, well, Zoe likes it when we're both on good terms. Plus, when Tania, Widow, Nikolai, and I can be together with her, she's a different kid. She excels at school, she makes good friends. I finally decided to bury the hatchet and put everything behind us. And considering there's another bun in the oven, it's best we keep it buried. You know?" I smile, already knowing about Rebel's big news.

"You, or Tania?" Sakura smiles, but I can see the pain crossing her face at the same time.

"Me!" Rebel shrieks, jumping up and down.

"Congratulations. That's amazing," Rebel goes over to hug Sakura, but when Sakura releases her, she looks over to me. "Try to come back tomorrow when he's not all up in his feels. It's been a rough day is all. I promise he's not normally like this. He's only hurting.

I need to get going, but it was so lovely to meet you. If you have any questions when you come back, I live in that house over there," Sakura points over to the one-story house with the wrap around porch.

"Awesome. Thank you so much." I reply as she walks off.

"So, do you want to come back tomorrow?" Rebel asks.

"Yeah, might as well. I need a ride, though."

"That works out. Zoe's going to get picked up tomorrow to come back to our place. I can drop you off around seven, if that works?"

I nod, "Yeah, thank you for setting this up. I don't know if I've said it, but I really appreciate what you've done for me."

"Oh, don't sweat it." Rebel comments as she walks back to her SUV. I do the same and hop into the passenger side.

I might not have gotten a lot of information quite yet, but I have enough experience to get me started. I can't wait to write about the asshole who bitches out a baby momma's friend. Chaz, you've just inspired a character in my book and I'm going to name him Tiny. The name is dual representation— his tiny fuse, and tiny dick.

CHAPTER ELEVEN

"To know what a person has done, and to know who a person is, are different things."
~ Hannah Kent

Chaz

"I heard you were quite the asshole to Rebel's friend." Sakura's typically soothing voice is harsh and accusatory while she comes up to me. I'm leaning against the couch while most of the guys are outside, enjoying the cool weather. It's nowhere near as cold as Montana, but we also don't have to worry about being frostbit down here.

I nod, not bothering to deny it. "Do I really get

called an ass for speaking the truth?" I cock a brow, awaiting her answer.

Sakura walks past the small coffee table and sits down on the worn, red-leather loveseat beside me. "I heard about it, how you essentially called her a slut."

I roll my eyes. Leave it to women to be overly dramatic. It's the best thing they're fucking good at. "She works for Crave. If I see a dog, it's a dog, not a kitten. You feel me?"

Sakura throws her hands in the air in frustration. "Why do you always have to be the blunt jerk? Jesus, Chaz. Not everyone who works for that company is part of their girlfriend or boyfriend program." Here she comes to this stranger's defense. That's just Sakura though, the best person to have on your side.

"Right, and the others take nude pictures of themselves and post it on that program they have. Fuck, Ripper has a membership and just showed me this girl ridin' a dildo on it the other day. Keeps beggin' Rebel to introduce him to her friend." OneEye is a great, safe platform for women to use . . . sure, but why am I the jerk for speaking honestly?

"Crina's working for the publishing company and needed help, and you were the one acting like a fucking dick. Take ownership for how you were treating her." Sakura grumbles, glaring at me with her narrowing eyes.

I shrug, not really caring to say anything else. "I know Cheyenne just left this morning, but you don't get to use that as your get out of jail free card. She's gone, Chaz. Accept it. Otherwise, you're going to destroy every good relationship you have here, and you know it." Sakura starts off sounding pissed, yet slowly eases her tone with me. Ultimately, she ends up sliding her hand into mine and holds it tight, pulling me in a way that causes me to direct my eyes back at hers.

"I wish Zane never wanted to start that clinic up there. I fuckin' wish she could've stayed down here, Sak'." I shake my head, more pissed than I'll ever let on. The fact of the matter is there's nothing I can do now, not with what I know, not with the life changing position I'm about to be offered.

Sak' leans her body against mine, trying to comfort me. "I know you love her, and it's okay to be sad she's gone . . . but the people here love you too. Promise me you won't ruin everything you have here because you're bitter that she left."

Poison walks into our view. I assume she was in the kitchen preparing a meal. Usually she is around there this time of day. She continues to stare at us like she wants to say something, but she won't. She never does. Always the silent observer. Shit, she reminds me of Dmitri from the Skulls Renegade MC out in Tennessee . . . always leaning back, observing. Fuckin' freaky if you ask me.

"What's on your mind, prospect?" I spit her position out, slowly reminding her of her place here. It's irrelevant. She can easily be replaced at any given moment.

"I'm only curious who Sakura's ol' man really is. You, or Mouser?" She snidely replies, keeping her glare focused on me.

I stand up, ready to tell this bitch how replaceable she is when Sakura grabs onto my forearm. She looks between me and Poison. "She didn't mean anything by it. Our relationship is odd to some people."

"Fuck what other people think. You're practically my sister. I fuckin' love you." I grit, shifting my attention from Poison to Sakura.

From the corner of my eye I spot Poison going to the front door of the club, and just as she opens it, a familiar, unwelcome face comes walking through.

Lucian Bane.

What the fuck is he doing here?

"Lucian?" Sakura belts his name out, not happy to see her ex- . . . whatever they were. Fuck buddies.

Dating. Who knows? It's a different story depending who you ask.

He turns his attention our way and comes walking over. As he dips his hands into the pockets of his pants, I notice how he looks even fancier than ever before. I know the man has money, but the small diamonds shining on his enormous watch tell me he's doing better than ever. I heard a rumor that the Steele brothers backed his cyber-security firm, which I'm sure only enhanced the grip he had on that business.

"Hey, we need to talk. There's been an issue." His tone is gravelly, putting me under the impression whatever this is about, it isn't good.

"Well, alright. Cut to the chase." Sakura stands, going over to him. She crosses her arms as she does so, putting on that metaphorical serious hat she's always wearing.

"My system was compromised, and when it was, many things shut down. One of which was the ghost software I had running on your mother's cellphone to make it appear as though she had fled to South America six months ago and moved your supposed whereabouts to the United Kingdom. Her cell officially stopped reporting to towers last week and I've been notified your father has booked a flight to Argentina, as well as Las Vegas . . . which is worrisome considering that was the last place Eduardo was known to have you ... correct?"

Lucian is right. Eduardo having Sakura here was how the club ended up offering her protection, though, she's a mess right now. Sakura is frozen in place. I can only naturally assume it's from shock, so I stand and head to her side.

A couple years back, Sakura left her family behind in Japan. Her mother was the leader of the Yakuza, which is pretty much the Japanese mob. Meanwhile, her father is the Emperor of Japan. From what I gathered Sakura wanted nothing to do with her family, and while leaving them was peaceful at first ... it quickly turned ugly. Long story short, Sakura's mother came here to Las Vegas and she was killed with her team of men. We were meticulous in covering our tracks, burning their bodies until they were nothing but ash, then spread them across the desert. And that was after Sakura found out her mother was the reason her older sister, who we all knew as Saffron, died. She was our deceased national charter Prez's woman.

Sakura nods her head and visibly gulps. "When did this happen?"

"Five days ago," Lucian quickly responds, shame evident.

"When was the flight booked for Las Vegas?" Her father shouldn't know where she is at all. We'd all went above and beyond to keep her location safe . . . though it's obvious he located her, and now we have no idea what we're facing.

"A month from five days ago. However, he already boarded his flight to Argentina. I have my team watching over their movements, but I felt it was my duty to come here and tell you everything face-to-face."

Sakura shuts her eyes, no doubt wanting to avoid this conversation from ever happening. "How did this happen, Lucian? You're supposed to be the best in the industry. How did this fucking happen?!" She hollers while pushing both hands against his chest in outrage. If I were her, I'd be terrified. She should calm down, though. She knows all of the Reapers will back her, as well as the allies she's close with, including her godfather, Eduardo. Luckily for her, he's cousins with the Mexican Cartel leader. If you ask me, she's got two powerful teams on her side.

"Are you even listening?! How did this happen!?" Sakura's holler turns to a scream and I find myself wrapping my arms around her waist, holding her back from getting to him.

Lucian wipes his hand across his mouth, visibly

showing the turmoil he's feeling. "I was hacked, Sakura. I was fucking hacked. That's how, 'cause I'm not the best, and the woman who is . . . she's my fucking protégé."

Sakura's body grows still and suddenly she stops fighting. "No. There's only one person you ever told me was . . . was even a fraction as good as you."

Lucian nods once. "Yeah, it seems Joanna outsmarted me."

"Fuck . . ." Sakura mutters.

"I thought about running the programs and ghosting as soon as everything got back up and running . . . but there wasn't any point. By that time, it was obvious he knew something was going on. I only wanted to come here and tell you what I found out, and that my team is watching your father and his men. We'll report back anything we find, considering it's the least we can do."

Sakura looks down at the floor and doesn't say another word.

"For what it's worth, I'm sorry this happened. You know it wasn't anything we ever intended, Sakura." Lucian speaks clearly, yet still Sakura doesn't speak.

"Thank you, for coming here and telling us." I dive into the conversation.

"Of course. If there's anything I can do, please let me know."

"Keep doing what you're doing, and we'll handle the rest." I tell him, releasing Sakura I escort Lucian out and walk him to his blacked-out SUV. I watch him ride off, scratching my head at how we're going to get a grip on this. I need to speak to Damon and Dixon as soon as possible, and in the meantime, I hope Sakura calls her godfather.

CHAPTER TWELVE

She is not broken anymore, she is stronger, wiser, and more beautiful than before
~ Relentless Woman

Crina

ALRIGHT. I thought I was going to sit back and wait until tomorrow before I went back to the club, or clubhouse, or whatever the proper term is . . . but I can't do that. The way that Chaz guy spoke to me was far too infuriating. While I did manage to write some notes down when I got back to my apartment and set my new laptop up, I knew I couldn't sit back and wait. He spoke to me the same way my father does, and . . .

there was no way I was going to stay here and fester about it.

So, I found out Tildi has a client who lives up around that area who she was going to see. I asked if she could give me a ride back to the club and she was all for it.

She giggles in the driver's seat beside me, "Are you sure you want to go in alone? I mean, aren't they tough and all?"

I scoff, trying to refrain from rolling my eyes. "I wouldn't say that. They seem like little bitches to me. Ironic how I have to write a book about them, right?"

Tildi giggles even louder, "I really like you, Crina. Something tells me we're going to be very good friends. But I do have a question for you."

"Is it about Gia?" I ask, dreading the thought.

"Alright, I have two questions." Tildi glances over in my direction with a smirk.

"Shoot."

"When you got back to the apartment, I overheard you filling Bea in, but nothing was exactly clear. Why're you so determined to go back? I mean, I was under the impression some guy pissed you off." Tildi looks back to the road, speeding up a bit since we're on the highway.

I take in a deep breath and relax my shoulders.

"This one guy there, he insinuated everyone that works for Crave is a slut. It pissed me off."

Tildi breaks out into laughter. "You have to be kidding me. You got mad at him because of . . . oh goodness, this is hysterical. Yes, we're all sluts and we know it. I'm totally fine with being called a slut, because it only means I'm embracing my sexuality, like I damn well should. So, if some idiot wants to call me a slut, I'll let him, 'cause I know the power I possess. You know, this dude is probably one of those jerks hating on Cardi B and Megan Thee Stallion's song 'WAP'. Please, he's not even worth the effort." Tildi motions with her hand and I listen to her words, realizing she's right.

"Okay, I get what you're saying . . . but I'll be damned if I let him think he can speak to me like that again."

"Now onto the juicy stuff." Tildi wiggles her eyebrows in excitement. "Why'd you think I was asking about Gia?"

It might seem crazy, but I feel like everyone knows about my past with Gia. We dated for a while and I was always around. After all, when you date a workaholic, when else are you going to see them unless you're the one making a massive effort. Looking back now, I know I shouldn't have done so much to keep our relationship alive, but I did. She isn't a bad person, but I know we weren't right for each other. Gia making the choice she did . . . it put the nails in the coffin that was our relationship. Though, it was for the best.

"Oh, nothing really. Gia and I dated a couple years back."

"C. C is for Crina. Oh. My. God!" Tildi shrieks, taking the exit off the highway. As soon as we're off the highway she makes a left like the GPS tells her.

What the hell? I must be missing something.

"What don't I know?" I question her.

"I've only been around for about a year now, but when I first started at Crave, the girls told me about Gia's ex, C. Said she was the love of Gia's life and she went into this depression after they broke up. Apparently, Gia went really deep into the rabbit hole because of something she couldn't change. Her family, I think? I can't remember it all, but I got the idea Gia's family was part of the reason for the breakup. But that could be wrong."

It isn't wrong. It's so, factually, correct. I had no idea about Gia going into a depression. Honestly, based on her personality I figured she would recover the next day. Not that she was an emotionless bitch, but she'd always been stronger than me.

"It's not, wrong I mean. Our families are a little different, specifically the way I interacted with mine opposed to hers. It was part of the reason for the breakup I suppose." I shrug, glancing at the GPS for a second. We're going to be at the club in a minute or so.

"Sorry, I didn't mean for you to tell me or anything."

Turning my head to look at Tildi, I smile. "It's fine. There was no pressure to answer, so no biggie. You can drop me off here though if you want. I see the driveway leading to their club now."

Tildi pulls over to the entrance of their driveway and I exit the vehicle. As I'm exiting the passenger seat, she leans over to look at me. "You need a ride home, too?"

"No thanks. I'll figure something out." I smile, confident I can get Sorin or Rebel to swing by and grab me. Worst case, I could call a taxi.

I slam the door shut and head down the gravel lane. It's only been a few hours since I've been here and yet so much is different. Where there weren't many bikes around, or vehicles for that matter, now there are loads. Man. Are they throwing a killer party or something?

I head to the building I was in earlier today with Rebel and push the door open. While I'm entering, I don't see anyone here. There are loads of motorcycles and cars outside, and yet, not a soul here.

What the hell?

The faint sound of a man's voice causes me to walk toward it, leading me down a narrow hallway with photographs of members lining the walls. Though, I'm about ten feet or so from it when I pass through the kitchen and spot a group of people in there.

"Whoa. Who's that?" A man asks then comes into the hallway, staring me down. "Who're you?" I see his leather vest has the term 'prospect' on the right, which is his left side.

"Crina, a friend of Rebel's. You?"

"Brick . . . either of you know this lady?" He questions to the group behind him.

One by one the people I passed file into the hallway. Eight in total, seven men and one woman. "Yeah, she was here with Rebel earlier. Her friend from what I can tell." The woman with snow white dreads speaks up. She's heavily tatted on her arms and I spot them going up her neck, and even on part of her face.

"Chaz around? He and I need to have a chat." I state, looking to the group of them.

"Yeah, he's in church with the rest of the guys. But if you wait a few, he'll be out." One with dark almond hair states.

I nod, though on the inside I'm furious. They want me to show an ounce of respect to the man who failed to show me any? I don't think so.

He has to be in the room with the voices coming from it. So, I head off in the direction of the hallway when my forearm is pulled back. I shift my body in the direction I'm being pulled in and see the girl with dreads. "Listen, lady. I don't know who the fuck you think you are, but I'm not havin' you walk in that room and fuck shit up for all of us." She grits.

Dragging my tongue across the back of my teeth, I'm furious. Is everyone in this place a total asshole? "I'd suggest you remove your hand from my body."

"Or what, sweetie? You're nothing more than a delicate flower." She laughs.

A delicate flower? I'll show her.

I yank my hand back, arch my hand and shove it up quickly in the air. Within a second my palm collides with her nose and a cracking sound causes me to smile. "Fuck!" She curses, covering her nose with both hands. I spot blood seeping through and oddly, my smile grows. The men around her curse under their breaths and meet my eyes.

"Now, this can go one of two ways. I can break all your noses while you try to grab me, or I can go see Chaz."

"They won't put a fucking hand on you, lady." The bloodied one tells me.

"Great." I turn and walk toward the room where the voices are coming from, push the door open and am met with a group of men with the deer in headlights type of look, dumbfounded at being interrupted, I suppose. This should be fun.

CHAPTER THIRTEEN

"She's a badass with a good heart, soft but strong. Unapologetic and honest. She's the type of woman you go to war beside— not against."
~ *Unknown*

Chaz

"Alright, I'm glad we could finally get everyone back to the club. We need to talk about a few things, but the first—" In the middle of Damon speaking the door to church opens up widely, exposing the face of a certain woman I called a slut only a few hours before.

I think my eyes are deceiving me, but everyone else in the room is fixated on her as well. Never, not once in my knowledge has someone interrupted church and got away with it. The chick walks straight in after scanning her eyes through the room, heads around the table, puts a hand on her hip and locks eyes with me.

Fuck.

What was her name again?

"You and I need to have a discussion, *Tiny*." What the fuck? Why is this bitch callin' me Tiny?

"Tiny, huh?" Cobra stifles a chuckle from his seat.

"Listen, sweetheart, my name is—"

"When did I ever say you could call me sweetheart?" She retorts while she blinks away, waiting for an answer. Man, this woman must be the queen of sass, and I thought that was Zoe.

"Alright then, bitch. Why the fuck are you calling me Tiny?" I rise up from my chair, snarling at her.

Damon raises his brows, not approving of my behavior but who fucking cares. It's not every day some pussy struts into church like she owns the place.

A smirk crosses her lips and for some reason I have a feeling like I need to be prepared for this answer. "I'm *so* glad you asked, and I'm sure your buddies here will appreciate it, too. You inspired a character I'm writing, his name is Tiny, and everyone will think he got his name because of his tiny temper . . . but you wanna guess why his name is Tiny? I'll take anyone's guesses!" Her smile grows wider as Mouser raises his hand.

"Tiny dick?" He sounds unsure, but the second I see her pearly whites I know he's right.

"Correct! Good job." Shit. What are we in class or something? "So, *Tiny*, I'm certain I'm accurately describing my muse. Your moody behavior only confirms you have the teeniest, tiniest dick. I don't even think it would classify as a micro dick because it's so small, just a little nub you can piss out of. Is that why you're single? Rebel never said you had a girl, and I mean, it would only make sense, 'cause of you know . . ." She motions with her eyes down at my package.

Damon isn't holdin' back his smile, and then I glance to Dixon and see he's snickering too. As a matter of fact, Widow and Boog have smirks. I twirl around to see Hawk and Kade, who look like they're both trying to hide their amusement, which I'm sure is only keeping this bitch going.

Taking one step forward, I try to intimidate the woman who's about half a foot shorter than me, and maybe sixty pounds lighter. If I wanted to, I could pick her up and throw her against the wall. "Listen up, bitch. Walk the fuck out of here and don't ever come back."

"Crina, right?" Damon interrupts me.

She turns toward him and nods, extending her hand as she approaches. "Yes, it's lovely to meet you . . ."

"Damon," His smile grows even more. "You're the woman writing about the biker club, which we all agreed we'd help you with. Though, I'm seeing you had some sort of issue with Chaz here."

"You mean Tiny," Crina doesn't hold back the shit eating grin as the guys all chuckle at my expense.

"Yes. Since you two have an issue, I think it would be best for him to take lead on helping you get this book out there. If you ask me, you two have some issues you need to work out."

Crina's expression falters and I start to laugh. That is, until I realize we're going to be stuck with each other. "Fuck. Prez. You can't be serious. I mean, stick her with one of the prospects."

"To be fair, we don't want to deal with her. Look what she did to Poison." Jolt walks into the doorway, revealing Poison with blood dripping over her lip, coating her hands and forearms.

"Jesus Christ! This is one bad bitch." Cobra cackles, loving this.

"Allow me to fill you in on what you walked in on, if you're open to it, for the book of course." Damon speaks to Crina, who piques interest in what he has to say.

"Of course. I'll take all the help I can get." She says, appearing to pay close attention.

"This room is where we hold church, which is where the club discusses important issues, and votes on them. It's a sacred meeting which gives you the reason for such a name. Only full patch members are allowed in church, though some clubs allow prospects in. The Reapers don't, because a long time ago one of our rats was a prospect and it fucked with the club. Since our national Prez took over, the prospects haven't been allowed back in. Anyway, before I get sidetracked, church is to never be interrupted, and if it is . . . the person who did it likely gets a bullet between their brows."

Crina clears her throat, understanding the importance of what she did. "I apologize profusely, if I had known it was such a huge deal, I would've waited to chew *Tiny* up until after he was out."

"It's quite alright, Crina. I believe we all got quite a chuckle out of your sudden interruption but do me a favor and don't ever do this again. I've given you a warning, and I'll have no problem havin' my ol' lady kick your ass to the curb myself. Is that clear?"

"Understood. Again, I'm sorry. I didn't mean any disrespect."

"It's fine. Now, would you be a peach and go wait for Tiny out by the red-leather loveseat? We'll be about ten minutes to go over some things, then he'll be out."

Crina nods, and leaves the room, shutting the door firmly behind her.

Out of nowhere Damon starts chuckling so hard he's put his hands on his knees. "Never in my life has that fucking happened, but man, did we all need a good laugh or what."

"Whatever you do, please don't tell her she can't come back. I need more humor in my life, Prez." Cobra belts, getting a couple nods of agreement.

"I'm so fucking annoyed. How does a bitch like that get in here in the first place?!" I snarl.

"She is Rebel's friend," Widow laughs, shrugging his shoulders.

Yeah, Rebel, the queen of getting her way. I sit back down and wait as Damon starts to speak again, informing the others about Sakura's problem.

"I'll get straight to the point since we have such a spitfire here tonight. Sakura and Chaz were made aware that the software Lucian had running was compromised last week. With that, her father established her mother isn't alive . . . we think. We don't know. What we do know is that two plane tickets were purchased. One to Argentina, and a second to Las Vegas in a month."

"He coming here?" Boog questions, getting an immediate nod from Damon.

"We think he is, but of course we won't know for about twenty-something days. However, we're gonna prepare for it. I've already called Eduardo and he'll be here in a couple days."

"Jesus, this is going to be a clusterfuck." Widow mentions, bringing his inner thoughts out like we all want to do. Only difference is, we know when not to talk.

"And here I thought things were going to be quiet for a while," Dixon chuckles, lightening the mood a bit.

"Anyone have questions, concerns, requests?" Damon asks the group, standing he walks around the table, giving us all time to think of something.

"One request. Make sure nothing happens to my girl." Mouser mentions, "She's . . . she's going through so much right now and I can't fucking bear it. Brothers, I need you to promise me we're going to protect her. She's lost so fucking much. She needs to know what she means to us, so, show her if you can. Show her by protecting her."

"You don't need to worry about a thing. Sakura is a Reaper and she always will be." Damon declares, "And if there's anything we do right, it's protecting our people."

CHAPTER FOURTEEN

Sweet as sugar, cold as ice. Hurt me once, I'll break you twice
~ Unknown

Crina

I'VE BEEN SITTING on this red distressed leather couch for at least fifteen minutes, being watched by the group of men and chick by the makeshift bar. The guy with the almond colored hair is pouring drinks, handing them out to his friends without a care in the world. Meanwhile, the rest of the group seems a little put off by my actions. Especially the bloodied one.

I think her name's Poison, but I'll have to verify that.

She must've slid her hand against her dreads, because now there's a faint red in her hair that fades out to a soft pink. She sits on the barstool, clenching her jaw while she taps her fingernails on the top of the bar.

"You seem a bit annoyed," I chuckle, speaking directly to her. I've never been the type who avoids shit. If you feel a certain way, you'd best just get it out. It's one of the things my mother hates about me the most— my determination to not avoid issues. It's much easier if you act like an adult and get them dealt with.

"No, why would I be annoyed?" She seethes, spitting sarcasm my way.

I shrug, "'Cause you didn't like your buddies witnessing you getting your ass handed to you."

Poison slides off her seat and comes charging over. I wonder what she thinks she's going to accomplish by getting in my face? Maybe it'll be an ego boost, or maybe she's only trying to prove herself to her friends. Either way, it won't be a good experience for her if she dares to put a hand on me again. Though, I thought I made that clear earlier.

From my right I spot Chaz coming out of the hallway. He sees Poison on her way over to me with a heated look in her eyes and grabs her by the forearm.

"What the fuck is going on?" He hisses, looking to Poison and then the group of men.

"Someone needs to teach this little bitch a lesson on manners," Poison grits, balling her fists while she tries to tug her arm out of Chaz's grip.

Chaz scoffs, nodding his head while he glances over to me. "I don't think you're wrong, but you won't be the one to do it. She's a friend of Rebel's, which means no one here harms a hair on her head."

"You're fucking kidding me, right?" Poison's eyes widen as she looks to Chaz in complete disbelief.

He releases her forearm as he speaks. "No, I'm not. Damon's orders, so don't fuck around." Looking back to the group of men, he clears his throat. "All of you fuckers hear that?" The group of them nods or confirms with an 'mhm'. "Good, now, go make yourselves useful. Clean some bikes, change some oil. Do somethin' that gets you out of my hair."

As he orders, all of them file to the door and exit the clubhouse . . . making me curious to know why he has such authority over them. I dig my hands into my small crossbody purse and grab my phone, unlock it and press the record button. I plan on asking questions starting in this exact moment, and I'll be damned if I miss something important.

"Why do they listen to you like that? You're not

their father." I ask, genuinely curious. It causes me to believe there's some sort of pecking order considering this small group wasn't allowed in the church session with the others.

Chaz shakes his head while he slides his hands into the pockets of his jeans. "It's their job. They're prospects, so they do whatever a full patch or officer tells their asses to do."

"Prospect?" What a weird term.

"Yep. Means they're like an intern, trying to get themselves a full position at the club, which means a full patch. It's the only thing that'll give them leeway, and until they're a full patch, they can't order around the other newbies like I just did." He makes his way over, taking a seat directly across from me on a matching couch. Though, that one doesn't appear to be as worn as this.

"So, what do they get for being a prospect?" My question seems warranted, though the way Chaz grimaces tells me he's frustrated.

"A place to sleep, food, people who will stand behind them no matter what. The club isn't some . . . joke or whatever you think it is. It's a lifestyle, and most importantly, it means we're all fuckin' family."

I'm getting the feeling he doesn't want to help me with this, so I have no problem telling him to shove it.

"Alright. You know, you don't have to be the one telling me all this. It's obvious you're pissed and don't want to talk to me, much less look at me."

"Lookin' at you isn't the problem, but when you open your damn mouth, I want to wrap my hands around your throat." His statement causes me to gulp, drawing in a deep breath. I don't know if I took that the wrong way, but it feels like he just said I was pretty, and then admitted he wanted to kill me at the same time.

Immediately, I shoot up and begin to walk over to where I see a couple of the other guys have sat down. Looking at them, I can see they were in the room with Chaz, or shall I call him *Tiny*? "I'll go talk to your friends, who might enjoy my company a bit more."

"Sorry, but that isn't happening. Damon told me to take lead on this project you're doing, so that's that." Chaz says while he'd risen from the couch and managed to get in front of me, spanning his arms out so I can't even go to the left or right.

"And you're doing what he says for what reason?"

"He's the Prez, so he makes the rules. All of us report to him. Now you wanna ask some decent questions or what? I'm getting hungry." Chaz's stomach begins to growl and I see he isn't playing around.

Glancing around the room, I see how everyone

looks the same. Rough, rugged, maybe even exhausted. "So, you said the prospects want to join because of having food and shelter . . . so does that mean you all come from really rough lives?"

"I didn't say that. You're twisting my words. Some of us come from the rougher side of the tracks, while others don't. Shit, come with me. I know a place we can eat that's about thirty minutes away from here. Plus, I'm bettin' you're thinking all of us have deadbeats as parents, am I right?"

I remain silent because that was my natural assumption.

"Yeah, come with me. You have a lot of shit to learn and I'd rather not have to be around you for a long time, so I hope you retain shit quickly." He grumbles, heading for the door.

"Do you really think I'm stupid?"

As he gets to the door, he places his hand on the knob and looks back to me, cocking a brow. "It doesn't really matter to me if you are or not. I just want you out of my hair as quickly as possible." With that, he pushes his way through the door and I'm left scrambling behind him.

Well, this field trip should be interesting.

CHAPTER FIFTEEN

The days that break you are the days that make you
~ Unknown

Chaz

"There's no fucking way." Crina's adamant about not getting on the back of my bike.

I glance around the area and know exactly whose cars belong to who. And I sure as hell don't see something she drove out here. "Do you have a grocery getter around here? Is it hidden or something?" I cock a brow, sure that if she drove out here, I would've spotted it by now.

"A *what*?" She furrows her brow and lifts her lip,

confused as hell. It's almost enough to make me chuckle— *almost*.

"Make a mental note, *folle*. It's biker lingo for car, a grocery getter."

Crina rolls her eyes, not maintaining any eye contact while she runs her hand through her hair. "This thing is a deathtrap and I'm not riding it."

"But you're going to write about it?"

"Yeah," She confirms, crossing her arms in front of her chest.

"Well, tell me this. How in the hell do you expect to do that if you've never felt the hum of the bike between your legs? Or the air against your skin while you ride into the sunset?"

Crina scoffs, craning her neck in my direction. "First of all, I have a vibrator for any hum I might need. Secondly, you sound like you could be writing this book, riding off into the sunset." She imitates me near the end, again, making me want to strangle her.

While she stands there, I mount my bike, slide my key into the ignition and start her up. Looking back to Crina, she's gnawing on her fingernails. "Are you gonna get on or not?" I holler over the sound of the engine.

"What?!" She yells back.

"Come on! Or are you just a little pussy ass bitch?" I holler, even louder this time.

The moment her eyes widen and she narrows her eyes, I know she's heard me loud and clear. She comes straight up to me and pushes my left arm with force, causing me to lose my balance, I land on my ass. Glancing up, I see her smiling as she gets on.

Fucking, *folle*.

I rise, dust myself off and get back on the bike. Turning back to look at her, I make sure to speak loud and clear. "You need to hold on, or you're gonna go flying."

"I'll be fine!"

Well, alright...

I hand her Kat's helmet. She hasn't been out on a ride with Damon since Luna was born, so I doubt she'll mind. In the meantime, I slide my helmet on after checking to make sure Crina isn't going to defy me right now too. Thankfully, she put it on and I'm ready to take off. I kick the stand and we're on our way.

At first, I take it slow, riding up the lane and turn onto the back road until she's a little more comfortable. We might be going thirty now and she's determined as hell to not hold onto me. On the highway that shit won't fly, so I speed up to about fifty, causing her to wrap her arms around me like she's holding on for her life.

That's better.

The sun's starting to go down and I'm betting within the next hour or so it'll be completely dark. We're headed to Boulder City for some killer burgers, and for Crina to see not everyone in the biker life is the product of the way this world can treat us. She has a common misconception, that we're all babies dumped on the side of the road, drug addict's kids, and god knows what else.

Only, I'm not.

We're headed to my dad's restaurant, *Boulder's Burgs*. He's owned it since we all came here to the United States, it being his passion. His father owned a café in the center of Paris, so I believe it's in the family.

After another twenty-five minutes we're here and pulled in my reserved spot. It doesn't say who it's reserved for, though, Crina's eyeing me down while I finish parking my bike. "We can't park here, Tiny, look." She points to the sign.

"Yeah, I see it." I grumble, taking my keys I slide them in my pants pocket and dismount. I offer her a hand, but she doesn't take it, leading her to fumble and almost fall. "I tried to help you," I murmur, unable to believe how bull-headed this woman really is.

"Okay, let me make this clear. I don't need your help, and I never will." Crina's tone is aggravated, spiking up a little about half-way through her proclamation. Which causes me to believe something is bothering her.

Before I can respond, she walks away from me toward the restaurant, not even bothering to ask me if this is the right place. Hell, I didn't tell her jack shit about where we were headed. At least I texted my dad before we left to let him know I'd be coming up, with a friend of the club.

Crina had no problem pushing her way into the restaurant, disappearing from my view. Taking in a deep breath, I head over to the eight-foot cedar door and push it open. The hostess station is directly in front of me, and one of my dad's oldest employees, Desiree, greets me with a huge smile.

"Charles!"

"Charles?!" Crina's reaction causes me to stifle a chuckle.

Desiree comes from around the station in her button up white shirt and black slacks, pulls me into a hug and presses a kiss on both cheeks. I do the same to her, looking into her bright emerald eyes. "It's been far too long my friend," I tell her.

"I'll say. What has it been, six months? Your dad has

been so upset you haven't paid him a visit, being so close and all." She grimaces, chastising me with a wiggling finger.

"Yes, well, things have been busy."

Desiree rolls her eyes, "No child is ever too busy for their parents. Remember that, Charles, before yours pass away too. If I could see mine just one more time . . . I would . . . just kill for it." Desiree sucks her bottom lip into her mouth before going back behind her workstation. "A date?"

"No!" Crina answers.

"God, no. She's incorrigible." I grit, glaring at Crina.

Desiree giggles lightly, "Okay . . . so your usual table then after you get changed?"

"I'm not getting changed, Desiree. He can either see me dressed like this, or we can eat somewhere else."

"God. You Beaumont men have to be so difficult. Don't you?" She throws a hand up in the air, starting to go off toward the back. I follow her and glance back to make sure Crina's behind me. She is, so we pass through the main dining area, getting stares from the judgmental older folk who normally dine here. Eventually, we're back in a booth in the furthest corner, tucked away from prying eyes and eavesdroppers.

"I'll go fetch your waiter. Would you like wine?"

"A bottle of dry white would be perfect. *Merci.*" All the employees here speak French, though I'm a bit rusty on my native language.

"Of course. I'll be back in a few moments." Desiree replies, walking off through the main part of the dining area, she disappears from view.

CHAPTER SIXTEEN

The only real elegance is the mind; If you've got that, the rest really comes from it
~ Diana Vreeland

Crina

CONCRETE WALLS, wooden beams, ivory tablecloths, and elegant light fixtures.

Everything about this place has me curious why we're here. Why a man like Chaz, also known as *Tiny*, and apparently Charles . . . is here. "Why did you bring me to this place?"

Chaz lifts his chin and puffs out his chest a bit, "I simply wanted to debunk your assumptions about bikers."

"Huh?"

"Not all of us come from poverty, or rough backgrounds. I happen to be one of the exceptions, so, here we are."

From the corner of my eye I spot a man heading in our direction. He too is in a buttoned-up white shirt and black slacks. Only, he has some sort of towel laying across his arm. As he gets closer, I realize it isn't a towel, but something to help him open the bottle of wine. "Charles, what a pleasure to have you here tonight. Shall I pour a glass for your father? Naturally I'm assuming he'll be joining you this evening."

Chaz nods, "Certainly. I anticipate he'll be down in a matter of minutes."

The waiter pours myself and Chaz a glass of wine, then fetches a stray glass from a nearby table. After he pours it, he sets the bottle in the center of the table. "Would you prefer any hors d'oeuvres?"

"What's on this evening's menu?" Chaz questions.

"Well, the usual. Your father prefers to stick to the best sellers. However, we have a pork rillette topped with apricots. Our classic cheese fondue, reblochon tarts with bacon and fingerling potatoes. They're a new personal favorite of mine, and lastly we have a frothy lettuce soup with onion custard to top it off."

I don't know half of what this guy just said.

"One of each, please."

"Certainly. Will you wait for your father before you order entrees?"

"Yes, of course. Thank you, Gaston." Chaz nods, saying what I believe is the man's name. He walks away and disappears out of view while Chaz lifts up his wine and takes a sip. It's crazy to me a biker is this classy . . . but then again, he obviously knows French. Maybe I do have quite a bit to learn.

"What's with the stare?" Chaz asks, returning his glass back to the table.

"I just . . . never expected you to be so fancy. You don't look the type."

"Looks can be deceiving." He snickers, and just as he does, I'm reminded about my phone still being on recording mode in my purse. Luckily for me it didn't go flying in the wind when he rode us out here, so I unzip it and grab my phone, only to find it's dead.

"Shit." I curse under my breath, beyond frustrated with myself. If I had just turned it off while we were riding, I would have a way to remember everything.

"Everything alright?" For the first time since meeting him, he seems somewhat genuine. I slide my phone back into my purse, zip it up, and then meet his eyes.

"Yeah, phone's dead though. I was recording my conversations so I could remember everything."

Chaz appears to be taken aback with the way he's narrowing his eyes at me. "I didn't think you'd be so invested in this to record conversations."

"Why do you say that? This is my job, and without it, I'd be homeless." Now I'm the one picking up my wine, taking a sip.

"You don't strike me as the type of woman who'd be homeless, Crina."

"Yeah, well, don't go making assumptions." I mutter, not liking the way he's speaking to me. It's getting to a personal level, and I'm only here to do one thing— a job. "You brought me here to prove I was making assumptions anyway, right? So, tell me what I have wrong." Okay, that was the perfect way to change the subject. Yes!

"Well, my road name is Chaz, which I'm surprised you didn't ask about yet. I already know you don't have any idea what it means, so I'll fill you in. A road name is a name the club either gives, or a nickname a biker is known by. So, Chaz is my road name, while my legal name is Charles Beaumont." He says his real name in a completely French accent, making me forget just who it is I'm having dinner with. Jesus.

That was kinda hot . . . okay, get your shit together Crina.

"Damon, your Prez. Is that his road name?" I ask, changing the subject so hopefully he doesn't notice how I became flustered for a split second.

He shakes his head, "No. Damon is his birth name, though he uses it as his road name too. Sometimes that happens, but very rarely."

"Well, look who the cat dragged in." An older man's voice belts, quickly getting closer. "How long has it been my dear boy, almost a year?"

"Six months, Dad. But leave it to you to be dramatic." Chaz replies, rolling his eyes as he stands to greet his father. They pull each other into a quick hug, kissing one another on each cheek. He keeps an arm around his father's shoulder turning to face me. "Dad, this is Crina. She's a friend of the club."

"We will discuss the club in a moment, but your friend is ravishing. Come child, let me see you!" His father smiles widely, offering me his hands, so I rise and he twirls me around. "Magnificent woman my son! Goodness. If only I were twenty years younger, I'd be chasing you without a doubt, *kitten*."

"Jesus, Dad. Stop with that shit. I said she was a friend of the club, *not* my friend." Chaz speaks up, glaring at me.

Well, it looks like we haven't made any progress this evening.

"Sit, sit. Gaston! Where are you?!" Chaz's father yells for his employee, and I sit as he's requested.

"Okay, I was starting to introduce you, but—" Chaz begins, though his father cuts him off.

"I am Timothée, my dear. It is lovely to make your acquaintance." His father runs his hand through his light brunette hair, smiling devilishly at me.

"Likewise," I smirk, liking his father more than Chaz.

Gaston shuffles his way over with a tray of food, placing it down on the table. One dish in particular smells like an absolute delight. It's a toasted bread with some sort of thick paste, and orange fruit. Wait. It's the apricot dish he was talking about earlier.

Timothée takes a seat closely beside me, presses his lips together and stares across the table at Chaz. "I don't understand why you need this club so much, boy. We left Paris for a reason, our homeland, and yet you want to be involved in the middle of trouble again. It makes no sense to me, but what bothers me even more is how your birth-father was killed for the affiliations our family had, and yet . . . you must meddle with danger."

What? Chaz is adopted?

Chaz flares his nostrils at his father . . . or adoptive-father's words. With a clenching jaw, he responds calmer than I thought he would. "This is neither the time, nor the place for this discussion." Chaz addresses Timothée, yet his eyes are fixated on me. Obviously, he doesn't want me privy to this discussion.

"Pfft, there is never the time for this. It's what you always say, you can't talk about it, it isn't a good time, you have things to do. This life will get you killed, Charles, the same way my dear brother died. I don't want this for you. I wish for you to live a long, long life my son." Timothée grabs the glass of wine in front of him and takes a sip, while I chow down on the crunchy apricot thing.

Oh, well, it's meaty. I wasn't expecting that.

Chaz cracks his knuckles rather loudly, "Dad, cut it out. This really isn't the time. Crina is—"

"Your girlfriend of course. I see the way you look at her. I bet one night together stuck in a dark room and you'd be at each other's throats . . . the best type of lovemaking." Timothée sighs, looking at me. "Oh, how I wish I was younger. You and I could've been something amazing, my sweet girl."

"She isn't my fucking girlfriend. Crina is a know it

all bitch who pushes all my buttons. The only reason she's even here is because Damon ordered me to hold her hand while she does research for her stupid fucking book. So, how about we stop with this shit, huh?"

Timothée claps his hands together, applauding Chaz. "Ah, there it is, the Beaumont temper. Although, it's interesting how it now spikes from you . . . when you bring such a beautiful woman here. Is it not?"

"I've always known you to be the type of bastard who thinks he knows everything, but, this isn't . . . this is not what you think it is. Get that through your thick fucking head. Will you?" Chaz snaps in a nasty tone, causing his father to be quiet for a moment.

I feel like one of those people watching a dramatic show on MTV, while shoving food down their throat. "Fuck this, seriously. Fuck this." Chaz rises, slides out from the booth and looks down to his father. "You can take Crina home since you're so fucking infatuated with her. Maybe you'll be a match made in heaven."

"Back to the club, I assume?" Timothée looks up to his son, further poking the bear.

"Yeah, something like that." He grumbles, walking away.

I don't know what the hell this was really about, but it feels like there are a lot of issues between these two. Although, since I come from a family who I'd say has high class . . . I understand it more than I'll ever admit to Chaz.

For some reason, calling him Tiny right now doesn't seem right.

CHAPTER SEVENTEEN

I avoid shit because I'm afraid of me, not you. Temper goes from zero to prison real fast
~ Fuckology

Chaz

I'M NOT much of a runner, but I knew more than anything else I had to get out of there. He shouldn't have said any of what he did, because it's none of her damn business. Fuck. I should've known better. I was simply stupid for even bringing her here to prove my point. But damn, my ego got in the way and I know it.

Even now, walking up the streets of Boulder City I sense my back tensing up, proving how I feel betrayed.

I made it clear as day Crina isn't my friend, that she

was a friend of the club. Shit. I even said it, just like that. He poked the bear once and I let him get away with it, stating again how she wasn't my girlfriend. I thought I made it crystal fucking clear but leave it to my dad to continue his nonsense. He was nineteen when my father was murdered, the only person able to care for me at the ripe age of five. I had other family, but my biological father didn't trust them. At least, that's what my dads told me. Truth be told, I don't remember much about my biological father. I recall the way his face was an oval shape and he had brown hair just like me. Otherwise, I can't remember jack shit. I was only a little kid though.

Fuck, part of me thinks I don't remember anything because it's a subconscious response, not wanting to have any tragedy lingering around in the back of my mind or whatever. I don't remember the car accident, but what I've always been told is that he was sitting beside me in the backseat when our car came under attack. How the men shot him numerous times, and the driver. I managed to unbuckle myself and hide under a blanket on the floor . . . which was the only thing that saved my life. I don't remember any of it, but it's what the police back in France concluded. However, I do vaguely recall being taken out of the car by an officer. Other than that— nothing.

A bench near the street is empty, so I go over and take a seat. If one thing's for certain, I'll never understand the way my dad is. He's always been a joker, but I suppose it's his personality. Pinching the bridge of my nose, I breathe in and out deeply.

Why did he have to poke the bear tonight?

Why couldn't he give it a damn rest?

Fuck. And he wonders why I don't come around very often. If he were to look in the mirror a bit more, he might understand.

"Charles?" Her voice startles me, forcing me to look up and see where Clementine is. She's walking down the street, walking her agonizingly annoying little dog, Pepper. It's this French Bulldog mix who yaps at every fucking way the wind blows. "I had no idea you were coming for a visit," She states in a peppy voice, walking right over to me. Her eyes shine brightly in the moonlight and her smile grows. She might technically be my cousin, though she's my adopted sister.

"Hey, Clem," I say, wrapping my arms around her. I hold her tight a little longer than I normally do, and in doing so, she knows something's up.

"What's got you so flustered?" She peers up to me with worrisome eyes, takes ahold of my forearm and pulls us both down to the bench behind me. Even Pepper joins us.

"Hey, rat." I speak to the little dog, scratching her head. She's black with rusty orange spots throughout her fur.

"I hate to break it to you, but she knows you love her." Clem says with a smile pulling at her lips.

"No, I don't. If it wasn't for you, I wouldn't even be dealing with her ratty ass." I comment, pulling my hand away from Pepper.

"Mhm, sure." She replies to me, then looks over to Pepper. "Pep, lay down."

Pepper immediately lays down on the other side of Clem. Of course, Clem now shifts her attention back to me, "First of all, you never come out here on a whim so I know something's up. You're being quiet as hell, and haven't once made a joke . . . so, wanna tell me, or will I have to pry it out of you?"

"Try to pry it out, kid. You're as terrifying as the rat." I mutter.

"I'll have you know this little dog has very sharp teeth." Clem giggles, leaning against me. She sighs heavily, "I know I don't say it much, but I've really missed you."

"I've missed you too." Clem and I fight like cats and dogs, but at the end of the day we're always here for one another. She's one year younger than me and has pretty much the same sort of situation with our moms. Shit, I can't even use that term. They were one-night stands that resulted in heirs as our dad tells us. We never had a mother in our lives, but it wasn't too bad. Even though he's a dick sometimes, I don't doubt the amount of love he has for us.

"So, what're you doing out here?"

"Eh, nothing much." I shrug.

"Come on, that's such bull."

"I let my attitude get the best of me and brought this chick out here to prove a point, only it backfired."

"Girl? Oooo, tell me more!" Clem claps her hand excitedly.

"No, don't do that. She isn't important to me at all. She's just a girl the club is helping do some research on her book, and she had this idea that all bikers are either poor or had some sort of traumatic shit going on in their lives."

"And you brought her here for what exactly?" Clem draws her brows together, not understanding.

"'Cause, she thought all of us had bad relationships with our parents . . . I guess. I don't know. I just didn't like the way she was insinuating we all had some fucked-up shit happen to us."

"Charles . . . you've been through some rough stuff.

Don't even deny it. Do you ever think for a second like it might've contributed to being more involved in the MC? I mean, I know why you joined. Or at least I think I know."

"The fuck is that supposed to mean?" I ball my fists up, feeling the need to get defensive.

"You make me want to rip my hair out sometimes. Don't play coy, though. We both know what being a Beaumont means, or what it meant at least. When your bio dad was killed . . . it altered everything for our family. Dad took you in, scooped me up and fled here to America. It was more important to keep us alive then to stay at the head of the mafia . . . for fuck's sake, Charles, we would've died in Paris. It's only natural for you to feel a pull toward that life, because I feel it too. Of course, I'll never admit it to Dad . . . but I do wonder what life would've been like if we never left."

As Clem talks, I can't dissuade anything she's saying. Everything is right, and I often find myself wondering the same thing.

My biological father wasn't just any average Joe. He was Jacques Beaumont, the boss of the French mafia, and he was assassinated. Even now, we still don't have answers about who killed him.

Clem's made a valid point, though. Dad's only

concern was keeping Clem and I safe, so he brought us here to the United States, and luckily, for the most part we've had an ordinary life. "You know I love you, kid, right?" I kiss her temple.

"I'm only a year younger than you, jerk." She jabs me in the side with her elbow.

"Still younger," I chuckle, causing her to laugh too, and even Pepper starts her yapping.

"Want to go grab some food? There's a bar that opened up downtown if you want to hang for the night. You can crash on my couch."

"You know what. That actually sounds nice. Is Pepper allowed, though?"

She whips her face around like I've just insulted her in some way. "Um, she is Pepper Beaumont. Do you really think someone could say no to this face?" She picks Pepper up and shoves her directly in my face. The dog wheezes and snorts. Hell, there might even be some drool.

"Yeah, I do think that."

"You jerk!" Clem slaps my arm and we both bust out into laughter.

CHAPTER EIGHTEEN

Lust rushes but love waits
~ Bridgett Devoue

Crina

I HAD to do a double take when Chaz first left, not really understanding the reasoning why he left in the first place. If you ask me, he overreacted so badly. Timothée didn't say much at first, simply sipped on his wine and made small conversation, avoiding the issue in general. Hell, Chaz just left me here with no way to get back to Las Vegas.

What a fucking asshole. I didn't think I could grow to dislike him even more, but man I was wrong. No matter what, everything he seems to do only causes animosity between the two of us.

"I'm terribly sorry for the way my son reacted. You see, he was never any good at having good manners. Though, I did try." Timothée smirks as he puts the rim of the glass to his lips and takes another sip.

"I'm sorry you're stuck with me like this. You must have things to do." I too take a sip of my wine, but it's only to ease my nervousness.

Chaz is a handsome man, but his dad, or uncle . . . whatever I should call him. Well, he really gives you the total daddy vibes. I'm assuming he must be in his early fifties based on the way his skin seems a bit aged. Though his crystal blue eyes compliment his golden hair.

Timothée shakes his head, "No, not at all. You see, at my age, I work when I want. So, luckily for you I'm off." He leans forward while a flushed glow adorns his skin, though I should've anticipated the devilish smirk that pulls at his lips.

I don't know how to react, genuinely feeling like Chaz's dad is flirting with me. "Yeah, but I'm sure you had other plans, not being stuck with your son's . . . assignment." There's no other word for me, or term that would be accurate. He made it clear as day that if

Damon hadn't ordered him to help me, he wouldn't be helping at all.

"I'm not. I'm having an intimate dinner with a ravishing young lady, enjoying good wine, and hopefully good food." It's obvious to me Timothée is trying to do his best to make me comfortable. What Chaz did, leaving me here like this . . . it didn't hurt as much as it would've if we were friends . . . but we aren't, so I'm fine.

"Thank you for your kind words, I appreciate them." I smile, taking another sip of wine and set my glass back down on the table.

Timothée grabs the bottle from the middle of the table and raises a brow, "Would you like another glass?"

I nod, "Sure, thank you."

"Of course," While he pours me a glass and then himself one, Gaston comes back over to our table.

"Shall I wait for Charles to return, or would you like to place your order now?" He asks, placing his hands behind his back.

"Charles won't be returning, so I think it's best we put in our order now. Bring out a chicken confit, steak frites, salmon en papillote, a slice of hazelnut dacquoise and tarte tatin." Timothée takes the liberty to order for the two of us.

Gaston nods, "Certainly. Any special requests?"

"A side of caramel and chocolate sauce, please. Otherwise, I'm sure we have plenty."

"Sounds good. I'll be back in about fifteen minutes." Gaston takes his leave and I'm left with Timothée who leans back against the booth, still smiling at me.

"It sounds like you ordered a feast," I comment, clasping my hands together on my lap.

"A feast? No. Merely a few options. After Charles leaving the way he did, the least I can do is give you a meal you can't forget. We were voted the best French cuisine in all of Nevada." Timothée boasts with pride, causing me to see how he genuinely cares for his business.

"Well, thank you. I really appreciate it."

"Stop with that, your thanks and appreciation. After the first time it's quite obvious you're grateful."

"Sorry, this is all a bit odd, being here with you. I suppose I'm not sure what to say. Chaz rushing out like he did shocked me a bit if I'm being honest."

Timothée throws his hand up in dismissal. "Oh, don't you worry about that. Charles simply doesn't like it when I speak about family issues, ever. He gets all huffy and puffy like the wolf that blew the house down in that children's story."

"Sometimes speaking about our families can be difficult. I for one had no idea he was adopted, or that his family was so close to him. Though, we haven't known one another for long. I am just a charity case for the club." I mutter the last bit, feeling a bit down on myself. Hell, Chaz doesn't have to be nice to me. I'm really only a task he needs to ensure is completed.

Timothée lifts his chin and cranes his neck to the side a bit, "The way you speak makes me think you've had some of the same issues— difficult family."

I nod in agreement, not wanting to get into my mess. "Yes, you could say that."

Timothée's eyes sparkle and he nods, bringing his hands together on top of the table. "Yes, well, tonight we don't need to talk about that. Instead, we'll simply enjoy each other's company over good wine and delicious food. What do you say?"

I laugh lightly, "That would be lovely."

Timothée grins widely, "Perfect."

I've never had a dinner this decadent, and whenever I was invited to my father's estate his staff had always cooked the most delicious meals. In saying that, Timothée's chefs have them topped by far. It's no wonder this was voted the best French cuisine.

It's been about two and a half hours and I'd guess it's around ten or eleven at night. I haven't even looked at my phone since dining with Timothée. Though, now I'm pulling it out from my crossbody purse and am reminded it's dead. Ugh, just my luck. We've finished off the entire bottle of wine and I'm feeling amazing, more relaxed then I've felt in the last few days.

Gaston has already come by to fetch all of the china on our table, and many patrons have already left the restaurant, considering they must've closed around eleven. Now it's only Gaston and Desiree here.

Footsteps cause Timothée to glance to the right. "Everything is ready for the first shift tomorrow, sir. Is there anything else I can do for you before I leave?"

"No, no. Thank you so much. I take it you'll escort Desiree to her apartment?" Timothée's eyes flash with wickedness.

Gaston's cheeks flush with a bright red. "Yes, sir. I'll make sure the young lady gets home safe."

"Good on you. See you tomorrow." Timothée replies while Gaston heads through the kitchen door beside our booth. Timothée waits a few moments before he speaks, looking directly at me. "I suppose I should arrange a ride for you, hmm?"

"You don't have to." I speak before my mind even processes what I'm doing, and with it, I feel my pulse pumping heavily in my throat. My mouth quickly goes dry and heat floods over my skin.

Timothée's lips part as he rubs his fingertips against the table, tapping away. "What do you suggest, Crina?"

Holy fuck. Okay. He's flirting, and man he's coming off strong.

I focus in on his features, knowing I'd romp around in bed with this man regardless based on his looks. His personality is simply a bonus to me.

Timothée slides out from the booth, stands and makes his way over to me. He places one hand on the table and leans down. "What is it you're suggesting, Crina?" He questions me yet again. I'm unable to tear my eyes from his, feeling my chest rise and fall slowly, thinking about his body wrapped around mine as he plows his dick inside me.

I gulp, watching his smirk grow. "We're both adults here, Timothée. Put the pieces together yourself."

His tongue darts out across his bottom lip and I rise, causing him to take a step back and peer down at me. Sliding my purse off, I toss it on the seat of the booth. "Fuck, you're a treat for an old man like me."

"You hardly look your age," I compliment him, snaking my arms around his neck I slide one hand up into the back of his curly hair.

His breath is heavy as it hits my lips and just as I'm about to make the first move his lips crash down onto mine. Only, it's not as rough as I figured. Instead, it's delicate, demanding, and sensual. Before long, his lips push past mine while his hands skim across my body.

I revel in the way his fingers tweak my nipples through my shirt. Breathing in and out through my nose, I take my hands from around his neck and fumble with his belt, savagely undoing it. His hardness presses against my hand while I undo his zipper, popping his dick free. It's wide, veiny and is sure to bring me crazy amounts of pleasure if he knows how to use it. I've never fucked a man this old, but I've heard they're the best because of their experience.

Timothée works at my jeans and shoves them down my legs, taking my red thong with it and spreads my legs. Within a second, he's hoisted me up and slammed my body on the table of the cleared booth beside us. He rams his cock into me with no warning and I moan loudly at the sudden intrusion, digging my nails into the wood below my hands.

Like a dog in heat, he fucks me savagely. So much that I feel his balls slamming against my pussy, slapping them. "Jesus, you're a wet girl."

"And you're a thick man," I grit while he grinds his cock against my G-spot, the last of my words coming out in a high-pitched moan.

Timothée places his hands on my hips, pulls me back to him and brings himself all the way out while shoving himself back inside. Over and over again until my core is filled with raging fire. "Motherfucker, I'm going to cum." I moan, grabbing onto the other end of the table I lean my torso down, giving him an even better angle to fuck me at, desperately needing to keep feeling this.

He chuckles with a shaky voice, "Good, me too."

Timothée picks up his pace and goes harder, ramming his cock into me like he's never going to fuck another woman again . . . and I come completely undone. My orgasm rocks through my entire body, causing my legs to shake dramatically. I physically feel my walls tightening around his cock, begging for more, pleading for more ecstasy.

"Fuck, yes. Take this cum." He snarls, digging his hands into my ass.

He stills for a moment, groaning while releasing his seed and slowly pulls himself free. Although, I figure that's the end of our fun. But I'm quickly made to realize it isn't as he flips my body around, shoves my shirt up and frees my breasts from the confines of my bra. He tweaks them like he was doing through my shirt. It distracts me enough that I don't realize his head pushing against my asshole until it's too late.

Just like when he slid into my pussy, he pushes into my ass in one swoop, taking me for the first time a man ever has there. Though, I sense he's going to take me for another wild ride.

CHAPTER NINETEEN

Your doubts create mountains. Your actions move them
~ Mel Robbins

Chaz

"What in the *fuck* is wrong with you?" Damon snarls, shoving papers off his desk in a blind filled rage. I'm pretty sure what he's asking me is a rhetorical question, so I don't bother responding. "Why in the world would you leave her in another city? I told you to help her, not freak her the fuck out!"

I cock a brow, "I'm not sure if we're talkin' about the same woman, Prez. There's not a thing that could shake her up."

Damon isn't pleased by my comment, glaring at

me. You know that saying if looks could kill? Well, I'm sure if they could I'd be a dead man right now. He grinds his teeth and balls up his fists, "I told you to help her with her assignment, but instead you left her in a city by herself, over thirty minutes away. And you want to know how I found out?"

Considering it's been two days since it happened, I'd fucking love to know. "How?" I cross my arms in front of my chest.

"Rebel sashayed her ass in here and ripped me a new one because of your actions. Tell me this Chaz, when have we ever treated women like dirt? 'Cause that's what you did when you left her there. Something could've happened to her. You never know."

I roll my eyes, not enjoying the theatrics. "She was fine. We were at my dad's restaurant and I knew he'd get her home safe. He pissed me off, so I bounced. There's nothing more to talk about."

"Nothing more to talk about!?" Damon's voice is louder than I've ever heard it before, and I'm sure he's going to stroke out at the rate he's going.

The door to the room opens out of nowhere and Dixon comes inside, shutting it behind him. It almost makes me chuckle. There's no point in shutting it, 'cause everyone is bound to hear whatever is said in here.

"You alright, Prez?" Dixon questions, looking between Damon and myself.

"Am I alright? Am I alright?" Damon repeats, pacing the room.

"Okay, dumb question." Dixon mutters.

Damon rushes over to me, places his hands on both sides of my chair and as he speaks spit flies against my face. "We have enough shit going on right know with Sakura's dad figuring things out. What none of us need is you going off and causing problems like this. I told you to help the girl, so fucking help her. Don't fucking leave her, don't fucking treat her like a clubwhore, sweet butt, club bunny or any other shit. You hear me? You treat her like she's your fuckin' ol' lady 'cause that's the respect she deserves."

"You've gotta be kidding me, Prez. She fuckin' calls me Tiny. *Tiny!*"

"Does it look like I give a rat's ass what she calls you? She could call you Flora and I wouldn't give a shit." I spot Dixon hiding his laughter from behind Damon. I know why. It's 'cause Damon hasn't had a blow up like this in a long ass time. "You get your ass over to her apartment at Crave and apologize like the fuckin' piece of shit you are. Go buy her flowers, a fuckin' teddy bear, I don't care. You show her that bikers aren't all . . . motherfuckers like you, 'cause I'll be damned if she uses the way you've treated her to paint us in an even more negative light. Is that clear?" He rips his hand from the sides of my chair and I give him a curt nod, showing him I've understood.

"Great. Dixon, do me a favor and suggest some ideas that won't get him in more shit with the club." Damon speaks in a completely different tone to Dixon while he's on his way to the door.

"Sure thing," Dixon replies, and just as he responds Damon has left the room, slamming the door shut. Once Damon has left the room, Dixon takes a seat in the chair beside me and leans back. "Man, you really pissed him off. I don't think I've seen him that pissed since all the shit was going down with Rage all those years ago."

"Yeah, sounds about right." Damon was a different man back then, filled with nothing but fury for what Rage had done to Kat. Fuck, the man did it to her mom too.

Dixon shakes his head in disbelief, "Why would you just leave Crina there like that dude? You know better. Fuck, you knew it would piss Damon off more than anything."

I sigh heavily, running a hand over my face. "Yeah, at the time I wasn't really thinking about Damon. Dad was pissing me off and I had enough, especially when he was throwing our family shit around and then referring to Crina as my girlfriend. It pissed me the fuck off. I'd never date a chick like that . . . with all that sass, fuck. I'd strangle 'er."

A smile pulls at Dixon's lips. "You sure you don't have a thing for her? Like, deep down?"

I give him a knowing look. I think it's been obvious as fuck since Cheyenne left, I've been irritable. I fuckin' miss her so much. "Brother, I highly doubt it."

"I dunno. I've seen some interesting shit like this, where dudes hate women and then boom, next thing I know they're married."

"I'm not the settling down type." I state, taking in a deep breath.

"I thought you told Cheyenne you would settle down with her if you knew you had a chance." Dixon speaks, making me cock a brow.

"Who told you that?"

"You're kidding, right? Indra was right outside when you two were going at it and heard the entire thing. Now, you wanna hear what I'm gonna say, or not? 'Cause remember, I used to be as bad as you with women."

"What, you got some words of wisdom or something?"

"Yeah, something like that. You're missing

Cheyenne, right, so go bury yourself into someone else's keyhole. Fuck your frustrations out. I mean, hell, dude . . . Crina isn't a bad lookin' woman. She's sassy, prolly enjoys some real nasty shit. I don't see why it can't work out. You help her with her book, and she helps you get out some frustration."

I don't buy it. There's no chance this could work. I shake my head as Dixon gives me an amused look. "Chaz, you gotta try something. If you keep actin' the way you are, you're gonna get your patch ripped off."

At this point I know Dixon is right. My options are limited and I need to try to make things easier between Crina and I. Maybe he's right. Hell, he could be wrong too . . . but only time will tell. I rise from my chair, "Yeah, I'll figure something out. For now, though I'll go grab her some chocolate and hopefully it's a good peace offering for her."

"That's my man. Women love chocolate."

I don't bother responding, knowing if I'm gonna do this I'd better get outta the club now. There's a lot of things I'd rather be doing and seeing Crina isn't one of them.

CHAPTER TWENTY

Toxic people will make you feel like you're holding a grudge.
No, dude. That's called a boundary
~ Unknown

Crina

I BRING the pale pink knitted blanket over my legs to warm me up a bit as Rebel goes on about her day. Truth be told I'm half paying attention. There's so much crap on my mind. I mean, I'm still reeling from the fact I slept with Chaz's dad. Numerous times in fact. Our night was a fuck fest and then he got an Uber for me and sent me back home the following morning after a big breakfast.

"So, I marched right in there and chewed Damon

up for how Chaz acted. I mean, c'mon, if that was one of the ol' ladies he'd have his hide tore up. No way was I going to let him get away with it either." She sneers, rolling her eyes.

I whip my head to where she's seated on the chaise part of the sectional. "I'm sorry. You did what?" I blink at her, finally getting pulled back into the conversation.

"Uh, were you even listening?"

"I zoned out for a second. Sorry, I was up really late last night writing. I downloaded a couple books from some big time MC authors to see how they structure their stories but based on my English degree and understanding basic story arcs I feel confident I'm doing it the right way. I think I went to bed around five this morning, I don't remember. But, I have about eight thousand words in my manuscript." I smile at the end, actually feeling happy with how much progress I've made.

"Man, you're really all over the place. You want me to brew some coffee?" Rebel rises, going over to the kitchen before I even have a chance to respond.

"I was going to say no, but what the hell. A good cup of coffee could really liven me up."

"Say no more, Rebel's famous kickers are coming."

"I thought you said you were making coffee, not alcohol." I joke.

She turns back and peeks over her shoulder, "You're a bit much you know, even when you're exhausted. That sassy attitude of yours never goes away."

"It's a signature trait. Not going anywhere, honey." I giggle, leaning back into the chair while Rebel goes through the cabinets and grabs the coffee grounds and filter. After she finishes prepping the coffee pot I decide to speak up, wanting her to pay attention. "Why'd you go and tell Damon? It wasn't that big of a deal, Rebel. I'm a big girl and I can handle myself."

"I know you can, but there wasn't any way I was going to let Chaz get away with that type of behavior. It was inexcusable, Crina." Rebel scrunches up her nose in absolute disgust.

Okay, I need to nip this in the bud right now. Rising from the sectional I walk over to the concrete bar in the center of the kitchen and lean over it, trying to appear relaxed even though I'm about to delicately stick up for myself. "Rebel, I appreciate what you're trying to do . . . but I can handle myself. If I can handle my family, I can handle Tiny Charles Chaz Beaumont." I snicker, hoping it will come off light-hearted.

"Crina, I—"

The doorbell to the apartment suddenly rings and I'm a bit startled. Tildi, Bea, and Fern all have keys to get in. They wouldn't need to ring the bell.

I narrow my eyes in on the door and walk over. "Are you expecting someone?" Rebel asks.

Immediately I answer, "Nope."

Then it hits me. It could be Gia . . . but I haven't seen her in a couple of days and I was hopeful we wouldn't have to run into each other very often. When we do it feels like nails are being hammered into my heart and pulled out, over and over again— pain and relief.

Preparing for the worst, I unlock the door and open it. Shockingly, it's not Gia. "Chaz?" I say his name in a surprised manner.

"Chaz?! What the hell do you think you're doing here?! Haven't you done enough already?!" Rebel snarls, darting over to the door. If I didn't have my hand holding it open, I'm sure she would slam it in his face.

He's holding a small lavender box in his hand with a deep violet bow around it. "I came here to make a peace offering." Chaz dips his left hand in the pocket of his jeans and pulls out a white bandana, waving it. "I surrender, ceasefire, and all that."

I'm not sure if he's being serious or not. So, I do the

only natural thing. I stare blankly at him while I try to assess the situation. Although, Rebel doesn't give a shit. She tears the cute box from Chaz's hand, trying to open it.

"Now, let's see how the dog chose to grovel." She snickers, pulling the lid off, she slides it under her arm and takes away the gold tissue paper, revealing pink and white chocolate covered strawberries. They have glitter and little candy letters on them, so I peek in a bit closer.

Rebel starts laughing, "Oh wow, maybe you're being legit right now."

Small little balls in a pearly white and baby pink are on the pink colored strawberries, while gold glitter and letters are on the white strawberries. There are nine in total, and on the strawberries, it spells out a message. Literally saying Chaz is a dick and he's sorry.

"I never took you as the kind of man who apologizes, *Tiny*." I smirk, feeling like this is more of a genuine offering. From the way his hands slightly shake, it makes me think he isn't happy to be here, groveling, and hoping it works. At first, I didn't like the way Rebel said she told Damon everything, but maybe it wasn't a bad idea after all.

"Yeah, well, when I'm wrong, I own up to shit. I

made you suffer because I was angry at my dad, so for that I'm sorry."

If only he knew just what that suffering led to.

"Peace offering accepted. Want to come in for some coffee? Rebel just started brewing a pot."

He runs a hand through his hair and scratches the back of his head, "I don't know, I mean—" Chaz starts to say.

"Don't even start. Rebel was just leaving and I'll make some Papanași while we wait for the coffee to finish brewing. Plus, you can tell me more of what I need to know about the club lifestyle and whatnot."

"Um, was I just leaving?" Rebel snidely remarks.

"Yeah, 'cause you're only going to stir up trouble. Pregnancy has just made your attitude so much more unpredictable."

"Dammit, fine, but give me the chocolate strawberries. That's the price you'll pay."

"Whoa. I bought those for Crina, and that shit wasn't cheap either." Chaz grumbles, glaring at Rebel.

"You either give me the box, or I'm with y'all for at least a couple more hours."

I swipe a strawberry and shove it in my mouth before I hand her the box. Breaking through the hard shell I'm met with a soft and slightly sweet interior, and then something else hits my taste buds . . . I think it's fudge. Good god, these are amazing.

Rebel waves and makes her way out of the apartment while Chaz steps in, and I shut the door behind him. Hopefully inviting him inside wasn't a huge mistake, but only time will tell.

CHAPTER TWENTY-ONE

Your apology needs to be as loud as your disrespect was
~ Quotes 'Nd Notes

Chaz

A DEEP SMOKY aroma fills the air as soon as I venture further into Crina's apartment. There's nothing like the fresh scent of coffee. I could drink this shit in the middle of the night and it still wouldn't keep me up.

"It was nice of you to bring the peace offering. Thank you." Crina speaks clearly while she walks around the thick concrete island to the coffee pot. Opening a cabinet, she pulls out two coffee mugs and begins to pour the coffee.

"It was no problem." I murmur, not sure what else to say.

"How do you take it, black?"

"You got it." I reply, smirking I decide to take a seat on the barstool. Crina brings me my coffee and hands it over, then goes to the fridge and pours some of that almond milk crap. At the sight of the carton I almost want to gag.

"I actually made some headway on the manuscript. Not that you care or anything, but what I've learned has helped me a good bit." Crina says, grabbing some mixing bowls and a few things from the cabinets. I know she said she was making something, but I have no idea what it is.

Taking a sip of the bitter coffee, I almost choke. Fuck. Who knew a girl like her would make coffee this way? "That's good, progress is progress. You know? Uh, how much grounds did you put in there?" I ask, clearing my throat.

"I didn't. Rebel did. It okay?" Crina asks, turning to look at me.

Shit. Well, that explains it. "A bit bitter."

"Knowing her she probably dumped half the container in. She calls them kickers."

"She could raise the dead with this shit," I belt, looking down at the black sludge. And for the first time since knowing her, Crina breaks into laughter. For the first time since being around her, I don't see a nuisance. I see a woman who has tons of spirit, good looks and might even be a little bit charming.

"So, *Tiny*, let me ask you some questions since you're here, alright?" Okay, now she's already knocked herself down a few bars with this Tiny shit.

"Shoot," I mutter, leaning back against the cushioned barstool. Though, I'm careful not to topple myself over.

"I've been doing a lot of reading over the past couple of days. They're fictional clubs and all that, but is there always some sort of criminal aspect to a club, or are there good ones too?" She begins pouring flour into the bowl and starts mixing away, throwing in lord knows what.

"Uh, it depends, I guess. I mean there are plenty of clubs who don't cross the criminal line, though they operate much differently than we do. I wouldn't even know what to say about those. Then there are clubs like the Reapers, where their people mean more to them than anything else. We're family, in a way. Sometimes we're the only family people have, and there's always gonna be people who make bad choices . . . so why not it be us who monetizes it?"

"Makes sense. So, I saw a lot where people are

heavily into the drug trade, prostitution, sometimes they're in human trafficking . . . but I have this idea, to do things differently. I want the President of the club to have a kid sister who was trafficked. I'm hoping to make his mission to save girls from the pain his sister went through."

"Sounds like a good idea, making him kinda like a superhero and whatever." I comment, deciding to take another sip of the sludge. I gag this time as soon as I swallow, making Crina giggle yet again.

"I'm not trying to make their club noble or anything, but I do want them to be well liked by people. The goal is to sell loads of copies, so hopefully I get something done right here. My boss, Victoria, she told me today I need to pick a pen name."

"A pen name?" What the fuck is that?

"Yeah, it's like an alias. Authors apparently use them for privacy and safety issues. Victoria said my last name isn't exactly . . . striking, so I need to come up with something else."

Alright. Now she's piqued my interest. "What's your last name?"

"Lazar,"

As she says it, I narrow my eyes because it rings a bell. I've heard this name before and I can't figure out from where. "Hmm, sounds striking enough for me. Where's your name come from?"

She releases a soft chuckle while she grabs a pan and puts oil in it. I watch as she turns the heat on medium-high. "Romania. My parents are Romanian."

Romanian. I know this woman can't be associated with the Clans. If she was, I would've instantly recognized her name. Though, I know of a Romanian businessman that lives at the North end of Las Vegas. My father had told me to steer clear of him and his sons. I know the chance is slim, but I ask anyway.

"Are you of any relation to Mircea?"

Crina drops the bowl straight onto the oven and turns to look back at me, with widened eyes. Mircea Lazar is a ruthless man and so is his father. I've never met the patriarch of his family, though Mircea came to Boulder City once when I was in town visiting my father. Essentially, he threatened to tell the new boss of the French mafia where he was. My father paid him a million dollars to keep quiet, therefore I have a bone to pick with that motherfucker if I ever come across his path.

"W-why would . . . how do you know him?" Crina questions with a shaky voice. Her eyes are wide like she's terrified.

"So, you are related then?" Go figure.

"He's my fucking half-brother. We don't get along."

"Who do you get along with?" I retort with a bit of attitude.

"Not many people," She grits, clenching her jaw. "Now, tell me how you know him."

"I don't owe you shit, Crina. Let's just say I'm not a fan of your brother."

"Join the fucking club," She seethes, turning back to what she was doing. I spot her putting some sort of dough into the pot and hear the bubbling noise as it hits the oil. After she's done putting the dough in the pan, she turns to face me. "Does this have something to do with whatever you left behind in France?"

Motherfucker. This is why I don't like it when my dad talks about our family business. "It might," I shrug. I'm not going to give her an inch because she's a woman, and she's the type to take a fucking mile.

Crina scoffs, grabbing the dish towel from beside her oven and wipes her hands off with it. She quickly goes back to ignoring me and goes back to the dish she's making. Regardless of her attitude, I'm not going to tell her something that's none of her business.

I watch as she pulls out the fried dough and puts them onto two plates, then scoops out a white thick substance from a plastic tub, and then does the same with what looks like jelly. She drizzles some powdered sugar on top and plops a fork on each plate before she walks over to me.

"Smells nice."

"Yeah, well I'm a good cook."

"It's great you're making some progress on the book," Right about now it's better I change the subject. "Any ideas for that name?"

She lifts her shoulders, "I'm thinking Knight, Black, maybe Fox. I kind of like Crina Fox. It flows well."

"Yeah, it does." I confirm, agreeing with her.

Jesus. How small does the world have to be? I'm having some sort of pastry dessert with the sister of the man who blackmailed my family.

"What did he do?" Crina's question shocks me. I look into her eyes and see the way she draws her brows together. "You can deny he did anything, but I can see it. When you figured out, I shared blood with him . . . you looked at me like I was the enemy."

I cock a brow, going for the humorous route. "You've been my enemy since the moment I set eyes on you."

Her mouth drops open and a glimmer shines in her eyes. She whips up her hand and the next thing I know, I've been slapped in the face with this creamy, flaky, warm . . . jelly thing? I think it's jelly. Dragging my tongue out across my lip I'm met with the sensation of sweet and sour.

"Game on, girl." I grumble, smearing my hand in mine I grab her by the hair with one hand and rub it all over her face, laughing when I notice it's gone up her nose.

"Oh. My. God!" She screams, looking like a damn purple ghost.

I hop off the barstool and break out into laughter. Though, I only poked the bear. Crina grabs the bit that's left on her plate and throws it straight at my face. It hits me in the nose and cream spreads across my nose and right eye. "Shit!"

"You're gonna get it!" I hiss, half laughing.

She breaks out into the same smile I was met with earlier tonight when I hear laughter coming from behind me. I turn and see a woman with fire engine red hair in the foyer, struggling to hide her amusement. "Do I even want to know?"

"Chaz, this is Bea. She's one of my roommates." Crina introduces us, so I walk forward and extend a hand.

Bea looks down and shakes her head, "No thanks. I don't want whatever that is smeared all over me. Nice to meet you though,"

"Likewise."

Bea walks off toward what I'm assuming is her room and I turn around to face Crina. Licking my lips again, I'm hit with the flavorful combination. "This is good, even as foundation." I snicker, getting another laugh from her ... and for the first time since speaking to Dixon, maybe he's right.

Maybe I can get along with her enough to get out some of my pent-up anger and frustrations ... but then there comes the issue of who she's related to. Fuck. Nothing in life is ever easy.

CHAPTER TWENTY-TWO

Family is supposed to be our safe haven. Very often it's the place where we find the deepest heartache.
~ Iyanla Vanzant

Crina

IT'S BEEN ALMOST a week since the food fight in my apartment with Chaz, who is slowly becoming more tolerable. I've witnessed him being quite a jokester. He's funny when I'm interviewing him, asking questions about the biker lifestyle and whatnot . . . but when we're both at the club and the other guys chime in with what they think about the club life, Chaz turns into a totally different guy. While he might've seemed like a complete ass in the beginning, I'm learning he's the king of sarcasm. And I mean, he can be a total dick at times so I'll continue calling him Tiny.

That being said, spending more time with him . . . I've begun to really fester about what he knew, and even more than that, what he never told me.

I still don't know what Mircea did to him, but tonight things will change. I'm at Sorin's apartment, sitting on the modern, black leather couch looking out through the window. Las Vegas is the most beautiful city on earth from the deserts, to the casinos, to the people.

"He's going to be here in five minutes. Will you tell me what this is about?" Sorin questions, coming into view with a glass of scotch on the rocks in his hand. He leans up against one of the metal beams and takes a sip, cocking a brow at my silence.

I don't mean to be so quiet. I'm only trying to think of what to say. Do I tell him about where I'm working? About being Gia's employee and then have to get pulled into that long, dragged out conversation on how it's a horrible idea. Do I say I work for a publishing company and I'm writing biker romance, and then go into how I'm interviewing bikers to have authenticity? Regardless, my options are limited. So, I say the only thing I can.

"He did something to a friend of mine . . . and I don't know what it was . . . but my friend said Mircea's name." I keep my gaze focused on the city, not daring to look at Sorin. He's always been the one to cut through me like I'm ice and I can't handle the questions right now. Because, maybe Chaz is slowly becoming more important to me than I thought, and after speaking to Victoria earlier today, she questioned on why I'd keep doing the interviews if I had what I needed.

Her question plagued me, like a monster coming out from under a child's bed.

She's right and there's no doubt about it. Why would I waste time when I could be doing other things? Because the reality is, I don't need to continue spending days on end at the club. Though, it's become a fun part of my new normal since gaining my independence from my family.

I've been told numerous times from Dixon, Chaz, Cobra, and even Boog how the club became their family. Little did I realize until today how they've already sunken their way into my heart. They're becoming my family and I understand what they all meant when in the beginning all I could do was imagine and empathize.

"You've gotta give me more than that, Crina." Sorin states in an irritated manner.

I shrug, "There's nothing else I can give you. I wasn't told anything else."

"You have to know something. Why would your friend say Mircea's name in the first place?"

"I was talking about something with him and my last name came up. Then he asked me if I was of any relation to Mircea, and his eyes went dark. It was like I became a monster, Sorin. So, I need to know."

"*Him?*" He questions, pushing himself off the beam he walks in front of me so I'm forced to look at him. "Do you have a crush little sister?"

"Don't be ridiculous. I'm only curious as to what Mircea did to paint me in such a light." I grumble, standing, I go over to Sorin's makeshift bar and pour myself a glass of vodka. Adding two cubes of ice I lean against the kitchen wall.

"And you think surprising him will get you what you desire?" Sorin belts, laughing.

"Yes. I do." I growl, frustrated beyond belief. Mircea and I might never have really gotten along, but the least he can do is give me some sort of answer. I have to know what I'm facing.

"Speaking of the devil, Mircea!" Sorin plasters on

his fake smile and tone, sounding overjoyed to see our eldest brother. The reality is I know he'd rather take his eyes out with a spoon than have to deal with him. Our family will be forever dysfunctional. It's one of the only things I'm certain about in life.

"Was I hearing things, or is Crina here?" Mircea's voice booms with authority as it always does. If you ask me, it's irritating as hell.

"Hello, dear brother." I come out into his view. "I'm so glad you could make it. Now, I'm sure you'd rather cut to the chase as well."

Mircea furrows his brows and looks between Sorin and I. He cackles lightly while he slides his hands into his pockets. "I'd love to know what the plan was tonight."

"There wasn't much of one, just a question. You hurt someone who's important to me and I'd like to know how you did that, or rather, what you did." I speak clearly, preparing not to back down from this fight.

"I've hurt many people, Crina. We could be here for a while." Mircea takes a seat in one of Sorin's chairs, making himself comfortable.

"I'm shocked you didn't just go straight out the door." Sorin comments, not helping the situation.

I shoot him over a glare. "Really?"

Sorin simply shrugs.

"To tell you the truth, I'm entertained. I'd love to know who Crina's fancied with."

"I thought so too, that she fancies someone." Sorin snickers.

I'm forced to roll my eyes, not addressing what they're saying. If they know I give that much of a damn . . . they could hurt him. I know Sorin would never, but Mircea is a different animal. "Who are the Beaumonts to you?" I ask, watching his facial expression shift from entertained to curious.

"How do you know the Beaumonts?" He answers my question with a question.

"I asked you first. Tell me." I grumble, not backing down.

"The Beaumonts were nothing more than an easy payday. I find it . . . thrilling to know you and I do walk in the same circles. What did you want with them, Crina? I doubt you do care, because you never have. If it's money you're after, I assure you our family milked that cash cow for everything we could. They're not worth your time right now. It's what you need, money, right? Guess defying father to prove a point wasn't your smartest move." A smirk pulls at Mircea's lips, and I'll play along. If he wants to act like a know it all, I'll let him lead me to the information I seek.

"Fuck. What happened to the money? I was told they had millions." I hiss, running a hand through my hair in an attempt to look distraught.

Mircea chuckles, "Oh, you're such a novice. Think about it, Crina, you're practically a child. Leave the threats to me. I told them I knew where they were and would tell the new boss in France if they didn't give me a million in cash. I had one of our people hack into their accounts, and I left them enough to run that restaurant so they weren't completely helpless . . . but, part of me wants to collect a payday from the French just because, I am growing rather bored these days. At least, I am until I leave for New York."

Boss. Mafia. They're associated with the fucking mafia.

Every conversation I've ever had with him is running through my mind. I'm trying to remember the smallest of facts and then it hits me. There was a remark made about moving to the United States. They fled France and now I see it clear as day.

"I thought they'd be an easy mark. I only wonder why they left France, still haven't been able to figure it out." I shake my head, hoping he'll bite.

Mircea places his hands on the arms of the chair

and rises, approaching me. "Oh, Crina, you have so much to learn. I can't believe this has happened to you."

I furrow my brows, "Huh?"

"Don't play coy. It's never been something that's suited you. You do fancy one of them and it's clear as day. Never have I seen more fury in your eyes, except for the time when you disowned our family. To have that spirit, there must be some emotional attachment." He scoffs lightly and begins walking off toward the door.

"I may have to inform the French now, considering you're deciding to make things a bit messy. I mean, you could just apologize to father and make peace with the family . . . or you could risk the entire Beaumont family's deaths being on your hands." Mircea turns to look at me. The corner of his lip turns into a devilish smile and I start to run toward him, ready to strangle his fucking throat when Sorin's arms wrap around me and hold me back.

"You can't go after him, Crina. Father is arranging a marriage between him and Bianca Petran. I'm so sorry." Sorin whispers in my ear even though I struggle, kicking and screaming.

"What will it be, Crina?" Mircea questions.

My nostrils flare as shakes take over my body. My

heart beats faster than I've ever been able to remember while tears pool behind my eyes. Chaz hasn't done anything to him, not one thing. Neither has Timothée.

There are very few things I know about the mafia, though I do know this— betrayal is often what leads to our demise.

I'm rendered speechless, trying to speak but nothing comes out. I only feel the dryness of my mouth growing greater when something slips out past my lips. However, it isn't a word. It's a cry. I look around trying to see where it's coming from when I realize I'm the source.

Begging. Pleading. Crying.

All for mercy.

All to leave them alone.

My brothers might think I'm a selfish woman, Mircea much more than Sorin . . . but I'm not the devil. And, after becoming closer with the club I can't imagine anything happening to them . . . even if that means Chaz, or his father.

"She'll apologize to father," Sorin speaks for me.

Mircea laughs loudly, shaking his head. "I hope she does. It's the only thing that'll stop me."

"She will. You have my word." Sorin promises Mircea for me and he disappears through the door.

Sorin's grip on me loosens and I whip around to face him. "W-why would you d-do that?"

Sternly, he cups my face in his hands. "Because I love you and these people mean something to you. I would never stay silent, not when it meant people you care for dying." Sorin pulls me into his arms and the moment he does, the second my face hits his velvet dress shirt, the tears pour.

CHAPTER TWENTY-THREE

The most dangerous woman of all is the one who refuses to rely on your sword to save her because she carries her own.
~ R.H. Sin

Chaz

"I APOLOGIZE PROFUSELY for being late. However, there were circumstances out of my control." Eduardo speaks, the rough tone of his voice making it obvious he's exhausted. Though, the dark circles under his eyes prove it as well.

"It's fine, friend. You're here now and that's all that matters." Damon tells him, pulling out a chair for him in the room where we hold church.

All full patch and officers are here, as well as the woman who we're here to protect— Sakura.

Eduardo is her godfather and used to be best friends with her father. However, bad blood went between them and now things are quite tense. Eduardo is sitting where Mouser typically does. He chose to stand next to his ol' lady, wanting to offer her the only bit of support he can right now.

"How can I be of help? I know it must be in regard to Sakura, considering the conversation we had over the phone . . . though important details were left out." Eduardo rubs his hand against his chin, sitting up straighter as he looks to our Prez. It's evident we're not the only people on edge.

Damon opens his mouth to speak, but just as he starts Sakura cuts him off. "There was a program being run by Lucian. I'm not a technical person, so I don't know the details, but I'll get to the point. It was imitating my mother was still alive, sending texts and pinging on cell towers. About two weeks ago Lucian was hacked and when it happened the program stopped running. My father knows something's up, and we were notified he purchased a ticket here to Las Vegas. So, he's going to be here in about two weeks."

Eduardo sucks in a sharp breath, "Fuck. This isn't good. Hiromitsu was never as callous as your mother, but, considering the events that transpired . . . I'm afraid he's a wildcard." Eduardo tells Sakura, then looks to the room. "What is it you need from me?"

"Information, and possibly a trojan horse. I know you and Hiro were once great friends. If you weren't, Sakura would've never been your goddaughter. Correct?" Damon questions, looking to Eduardo.

Eduardo nods. "You are correct, although, things have changed drastically through the years. Keeping her safe and away from her parents was my goal when I asked for your help . . . and in doing so, I made things much worse between us."

"My mother was the only person to blame, and you know it." Sakura speaks in an angered voice. She clears her throat, "We found out how she really felt about my father that night in the desert. She called him a feeble fool, said she was the brains of the operation. I didn't know this back then, but I realize it now . . . you were protecting me from my mother, not my father. She was the dangerous one. We all witnessed it firsthand."

I don't say a word, knowing it's not my place. I could say how her mother was a crazy bitch, but we all know it's true. If you ask me, her father will want vengeance for what was done . . . which I'm sure he doesn't *know* about just yet. Though, he's on his way to figuring it out.

"How the fuck did this happen?" Eduardo grumbles, showing the only bit of emotion since being here. "Shouldn't that rotten ex of yours have a back-up system or something?" Eduardo shifts his attention to Sakura.

"Why ask questions like this now? It won't do us any good. I understand you're frustrated, but there's nothing that can be done at this point." Sakura gently informs him.

"Sakura is right, and it's why we're preparing for the worst. Your mother was the more dangerous one, however your father is an unpredictable wildcard. We don't know how he feels or what he thinks about your mother's . . . disappearance." Damon speaks up, addressing the room.

"He knew nothing about my sister's death. Remember? She made it seem like he had no idea." Sakura speaks, though I'm not sure if she's speaking directly to Damon or her godfather.

Amara, who is now the Prez of our Chihuahua charter, shot Sakura's mom before her mother killed her. She was about to end her daughter's life after she already murdered Sakura's oldest sister in cold blood. Actually, she didn't even do it. She paid a rival MC club in Montana to kill Saffron, who was our former national

Prez's woman. The fucked-up part is that Saffron had a little girl named Sydney, and shortly after her death, her man died. His name was Fist and he was the national charter Prez. Sydney was left with no one and his daughter, Ashley took her in for a while until Zane, her brother and his wife, Octavia, formally adopted the girl.

She must be about sixteen now. Shit. Kids grow up so quickly. I remember when she was an annoying, bratty little eight-year-old.

"Do you think that will protect you?" Mouser asks, though not in a nice manner.

Sakura turns her head to look at him in shock, like the rest of us.

"Fuck, I'm sorry. I just don't think trying to be optimistic and think your father isn't going to kill you for what we've all done is going to help. If you tell him Saffron was murdered by your mother, it's only going to piss him off more and he'll be even more unpredictable."

Sakura begins to open her mouth, but Eduardo cuts her off. "Your husband is right."

"He isn't my husband," Sakura whips her head to her godfather and glares.

From where I'm seated, I watch as Mouser kneels on the ground while Sakura is distracted and pulls out a giant gold box from his back pocket. Shit, he was acting totally normal and everything.

"Maybe we should change that," Mouser speaks with a shaky voice, showing every brother in this room he's nervous as all hell. He opens the box and a light shines on a ring that could blind me from here.

Sakura turns back to face him with furrowed brows, about half ready to give him an earful when she realizes what's happening. Fuck, I didn't think this was a good idea at first . . . but as the days passed and Sakura made it more and more obvious how fearful she is I might've put a bug in Mouser's ear. He's had this ring for a year and kept saying he was waiting for the right moment, the right time, all that bullshit.

I went off on him a couple days ago and said there would never be a right time, so to tell the people you love more than anything now, and not later on.

"W-what are y-you doing?" Sakura asks with a high-pitched voice.

Widow begins chuckling and I shoot him a glare that tells him how much I'll fuck him up if he ruins this moment for her. I look across the table for a second and see Dixon is giving him a warning as well.

"I'm asking the woman I love more than anything if she'll be my wife, 'cause we've damn near endured the impossible time and time again, and I want you to know how much I love you Sakura. Enough to lock you down forever and spend every remaining day I have on this Earth with you. Now, will you stop makin' me sweat bullets and tell me if you're going to marry me or not?" Even from a few feet away I can see the sweat beading at his hairline. Even his face is flushing with red and pink blotches from his nervousness.

"Is this real?" She mutters, bringing a hand up over her mouth. It shakes drastically and I spot her other hand doing the same thing. Shit, she's in shock.

"Yes, it's real, Sak'! Now give the man an answer before he shits himself." I laugh, giving her the extra push she needs.

Sakura nods her head eagerly, "Yes. Yes, I'll marry you!"

Mouser slides the glitzy ring onto her ring finger and rises, lifting her up in the air and landing a slammer down onto her lips.

"We needed something happy to bring us together around here." Cobra chuckles.

"Yeah, it was about damn time." Damon pipes up. "Now, we have some time so we need to figure out a solid plan. I don't want us to be caught off guard at all. Dixon, can you reach out to Lucian and find out if anything else has come up?"

"Yep. I'll call him when church ends and give you a status update."

"Awesome. Thank you. The last thing we need is to have shit blow up down here again. Not when Montana's already having a couple issues."

Everyone pays close attention to Damon since he finished speaking. "What kind of problems are going on up there?" I'm the only one with enough balls to ask.

"It appears Cheyenne's brother isn't exactly happy she's working with the Reapers, considering she didn't want anything to do with the Corrupt Kings and all."

I shut my eyes for a moment, not able to push back the worry I'm feeling for her . . . but it comes in waves. Though, at the end of the day I know she can handle her brother, because Chey' is the type of woman who can handle any man who steps in her path.

CHAPTER TWENTY-FOUR

A queen will always turn pain into power
~ @Visual.Sin

Crina

"I HEARD they're having a party tonight, so, you sure you wanna stay overnight?" Rebel asks from beside me. I once again asked her to bring me over to the club, preferring her company over an Uber driver.

"A party? They celebrating something?" I question, a bit curious. Rebel has told me about the notorious biker parties she took part in her early twenties, but I've never had the pleasure of being at one myself.

"Rumor has it, Sakura and Mouser are engaged, though, I don't have confirmation."

"Well, how do you know that?"

"One of the bunnies told me," Rebel says, making a right on the road that leads up to the club's driveway. The bunnies are what we call the girls that work at the Bad Bunnies brothel, which is owned by the club. It's probably one of the only legal forms of income the club has to be honest. I don't know about their other business practices, but I know better than to ask. "Who. What the hell?" Rebel's sudden tone of voice change causes me to stop looking at my phone, and as I glance up, I see a group with metal posts and chain link fencing.

As we get closer, I see it's the prospects and not the full patches. "I'm not shocked in the least bit it's the prospects doing that." Though, I'm unable to hold back my laughter.

"Damn straight. None of the others would be out here busting their asses." Rebel giggles alongside me and flies past them.

She drives right up to the clubhouse and parks her monster of an SUV. "Will you need a ride tomorrow, or is Chaz going to drop you back off?" Rebel asks as she opens the door. I slide out of the passenger side and walk around the other side of the vehicle.

"I think he'll drop me off. Things have been a bit better between us since he cam—"

"The food incident. Oh, I heard." Rebel smirks.

I for one didn't tell her a thing about it. "Uh, what the hell? Who told you?"

"Widow. Guess Chaz came back here and told the guys about it." Rebel starts walking over to the club door and it comes open almost on its own, but then we spot Indra behind it. She's Dixon's ol' lady, and the sweetest woman part of this club. She even teaches yoga and meditation to some of us. I took a class a few days ago and it was amazing.

"Hey! You coming to class on Saturday morning?" Indra chuckles.

"Morning? How early we talking?" I question.

"Ten or so." Indra replies, then looks to Rebel. "You know, you should come too. It would be great for that little one."

"I'll think about it." Rebel replies while venturing further inside the club. She came out here to pick up Zoe since Widow and Tania have had her for a couple days.

"Do me a favor and talk her into it. She'll be grateful when labor comes if she starts doing this now. Yoga helped me so much when it came to Khloe's birth." Indra tells me, placing a hand on my shoulder as she walks by.

I call back to her, "I make no promises!"

She laughs lightly and I decide to go into the club until I realize I left my laptop back in the car. So, I rush back over and open the passenger door, yanking out my tan laptop bag and sling it over my shoulder. It has my wallet in the inside pocket incase I need it.

I get back in the club and go to my usual red-leather loveseat. It's kind of my zone, or my favorite writing chair. I'm not sure which, but lately I've gotten more words written here than I have at the apartment. I'm starting to think it's because I'm in the element of my book and being here helps inspire me.

I open my laptop and instantly open up my word document. I've been writing so fast I can hardly believe it. In the bottom left hand corner, it tells me I'm at 104 pages with almost forty-thousand words. Man, that does a lot to motivate a girl.

Taking my blue screen glasses from my laptop, I slide them on and read the last bit of what I'd written early this morning.

He climbed on top of her, staring right into her ever-green eyes and cupped her face in his hands. "When will you get this through your thick head? I will do anything for you, Katrina. I'll climb every mountain, slaughter anyone who tries to harm you, I'll do anything to prove how much I care about you."

Katrina knew Tiny had these feelings for her but given

her past there were things that haunted her far greater than he could ever understand. "Trevor." *She used his legal name to show the seriousness in her tone.* "You deserve someone better than me. Some woman who isn't damaged. I'm . . . I'm no good for you."

Tiny slammed his fist through the wall in one foul swoop, angered by how Katrina always seemed to search for an excuse. He placed his forehead against hers and stared into her eyes, breathing deeply, slightly shaking his head. "No. I'm not going to give up on this. I'm not going to give up on us, 'cause I know we can be something great."

His words made Katrina's heart swell ten times the size, although at the same time she felt like she was being ripped apart. She wanted Trevor, but she was terrified to commit to him. She felt like all the demons from her past would come running in and he'd regret making these claims of adoration.

"Trevor, this would never work. You and I are from two different lives. For fuck's sake, we hated each other."

He nodded his head in agreement, "Yeah, we did hate each other . . . but we don't now. Fuck!" *Tiny slammed his lips onto Katrina's out of nowhere and while she tried to fight it, she ultimately gave in, welcoming the feeling of his lips against hers.*

"Hey. I didn't see you sneak in here," Chaz says, causing me to jump. I end up tossing my laptop and he catches it, plasters a sinful smile on his face and turns it around. "Damn, what're you hiding on this?"

He turns his body away from mine and pure fear strikes through me. I stand up and try to paw at the laptop, but he turns his body the alternate direction so I can't grab it. "Chaz, please, give me that."

"No way. I wanna see what freaked you out so ba —. Whoa. Wait a second. Didn't you name this one dude after me?" Chaz finally turns around, but he's sporting a shit eating grin. "This is me, isn't it?"

He licks his bottom lip and I don't say a word. 'Cause he already knows. Fuck.

Chaz takes a step closer to me, plops my laptop on the loveseat and looks down into my eyes. "You have something to tell me, Crina?"

CHAPTER TWENTY-FIVE

She never cared for the crown. She preferred the sword.
~ R.H. Sin

Chaz

THE MOMENT I ASK HER, her cheeks flush with a bright cherry red. She starts shuffling her feet and tries to speak in a weak tone, barely getting a word out. "I . . . um . . . I just . . . it's just a book."

Scoffing lightly, I think it's adorable how she's trying to pass this off as just being her work. Since she shoved that Romanian dessert in my face, we've gotten along better than we ever have. Maybe it was the climax we both needed to see we weren't bad people, just strong willed and bullheaded.

"Crina, don't lie to me." I can't hide how much I'm enjoying this. For the first time since Cheyenne has been gone, I felt amazing. Actually, if I'm being honest it happened at the food fight. I was torn into the present and had no time to think about the past. Just like I am right now.

She lowers her eyes and takes a gulp, desperately trying to figure out how she can get out of this. "I don't know what you're thinking, Chaz, but I can assure you it's not what you think."

I glance down for a split second and see her nipples peeking through her thin white t-shirt. Taking a step forward, I back her into the wall and bring my hand up, skirting it across her hardened nipples. "What's this, then?" I speak in a whisper, telling her in my tone how I know what game she's playing.

Her cheeks flush even brighter. Bingo. I'm right. She has a fucking crush on me.

"I don't want to mix things, not when we got off on the wrong foot and we're just starting to get along. Sex could complicate things. And that's the last thing I want. We've had enough complications, don't you think?" She finally brings her eyes up to look at me and I smirk, brushing a stray hair behind her ear.

"Crina, you and I are always going to be complicated. There's no doubt about it in my mind. But fine, I'll back off . . . for now."

"For now?" She draws her brows together, giving me a confused look.

"Yep. Tonight, you can see how we party, and you can ask more questions if you have any." I tell her. Backing away I head over to the loveseat and put her laptop in the bag. "No more writing tonight. Tonight, is for having fun."

"You're not my boss." She obviously points out.

"No, I'm not . . . but if I'm not mistaken, you're incredibly ahead of schedule. Plus, if you want to write about a club party then you need to be present. I'll go put your laptop up in my trailer. In the meantime, get a drink and loosen up a bit."

I leave with her shit before she can so much as try and fight me on it. One thing I've started to realize about Crina is how she isn't the type who ever backs down. She will fight tooth and nail for what she wants or desires, and it's one of the few traits I admire about her.

As I walk out of the club with her bag, I think about the day I got my ass chewed out by Damon and how Dixon told me Crina and I might be good fuck buddies or whatever. I thought about it for a bit, and yeah, we'd probably be fucking amazing fuck buddies .

.. but I've never been that type of dude. I'm typically a hit it and quit it type of guy. The only exception was Amara, but for a minute I thought her and I were gonna start dating. It didn't happen, but hey, we were both satisfied so no harm done.

I paid attention to what Dixon was *really* saying, poking at the fact Crina and I are similar. As far as our personalities go at least. I'd never met a woman like that, the female version of myself that is. It makes me curious, even to this day. I hadn't acted on anything as of yet, but given what I found on her laptop, she's fucked.

Literally and metaphorically.

I'll be ramming my cock into her heat tonight, and that's a fact.

Darting up the stairs, I push open my door and take her laptop back to my bedroom, setting it right at the bottom of the bed, directly beside my dresser. This way if anyone does have the balls to wander in here tonight, they won't be able to find it easily.

I turn and head out of the trailer, making my way back to the club. When I get there, I spot Crina chatting with Izzy, Cobra's girlfriend. She's Cobra's girlfriend. I'm pretty sure he made her his ol' lady, but Izzy keeps givin' him shit about not having her own cut like some of the other biker clubs do. She stirred up so much of a ruckus, Cobra went to Damon to get cuts made for the women who are ol' ladys . . . but we ended up getting them for the girlfriends too. I mean, that shit really doesn't matter around here. If one of us is dating someone, you sure as fuck better treat that woman like she's a brother's ol' lady. Otherwise, your body might get buried in the middle of the desert.

This is why I invited Crina to the club tonight, 'cause I wanted her to see this shit, to see what ol' men do for their women. If she's gonna keep up this writing stuff, she sure as fuck better have it be accurate.

It's a bit past eight and I just saw Rebel take Zoe out, which means we can really get rowdy now. Mirage and Cirque are doing the moms here a favor and watching the kiddos so the women could have a night to decompress. If you ask me, they don't get enough of it.

"Who's ready for a damn good time?!" Widow belts, chuckling like the damn devil. Now this guy is someone who can stir up some shit when he's drunk. One time, Hawk and I had to tear his ass off a mechanical bull when we went on a run to Texas. Funniest shit of my life.

Damon's sitting in the corner with Kat on his lap, and she's smiling more than she has in a while. She'd been through some serious shit all those years ago but being with Damon and having Luna has really turned her life around. It makes me happy for them. I figure we're gonna have to wait a while for everything to go down, so I walk up to Crina and wrap my arm around her waist.

I can feel her eyes bearing into me, but I won't let it bother me. 'Cause lord knows she needs to get used to it. Once I see something I like, I hardly give up easily.

CHAPTER TWENTY-SIX

All she wanted was the effort she gave
~ R.H. Sin

Crina

IT'S WELL past ten now according to the clock on the club wall. Then again, who knows when the last time the batteries were changed. Upon first glance I don't see any of these guys as the fixer upper type. Sure, they could help you with your car, bike, or scooter . . . but changing a lightbulb? Eh, I don't think so.

I've already had three grape wine coolers at this point, and I'm ready for another. Warmth pools in my belly and all my worries have faded away. Just as it should be.

"If you have anymore questions to ask, you'd better do it now before we're both fucked up." Chaz chuckles from beside me, his hand still on my hip.

I peer up and smile at him from where we stand in the club. We're off by ourselves after Cobra took Izzy away to go dance to *Midnight Sky* by Miley Cyrus. We'd chatted with Indra and Dixon for a while after that but now we find ourselves alone. Raven and Hawk came over to say hi, but they've been really quiet the past couple days. I'm not sure what's going on with those two, but I don't dig unless people want to tell me.

"Fine, but I'm only asking because you told me to, and I've read some books where this is the case." Immediately, Chaz raises an eyebrow in curiosity. "Is there some sort of trauma, or traumatic events that lead people to this lifestyle?"

He removes his hand from around my waist and crosses his arms in front of his chest. "What do you mean? Like shit we've been through in life? The tough shit?"

I nod, then shrug. "Yeah, I think so. Like, has there been anything super difficult for anyone here?"

"I'm not gonna go around talking about other people's business, but I can tell you the club saved my life when I was going through some . . . hard times. I don't talk about it much, not hardly ever, but it's 'cause it's not light shit. Seeing as you were honest with me about your identity, I'm going to tell you, and I'm going to do it before I change my mind."

I start to speak but Chaz puts his hand up to silence me and I notice something I've never really paid attention to before. He has scars, lines going up and down, and even across. God. How did he get scars like that? "Crina, don't. Seeing that shit on your laptop earlier made it evident we sorta dig each other, so, I'm gonna tell you this now and hope it won't hurt as much as it does while I'm sober. My wife killed herself. It happened almost ten years ago now, but I got her pregnant when we were teenagers. Instead of aborting, we decided to keep it. It was picture perfect for a while, until we were around twenty-something weeks. Went in for a regular ultrasound and our little boy didn't have a heartbeat anymore. Eli." Chaz smiles, pausing for a moment before he continues.

"We found out on the fourth floor of the hospital. That's where her OBGYN was. After we found out, she said she needed some air. So, she went out onto this rooftop area. I gave her ten minutes to breathe, give her the time she needed by herself, without me hovering . . . but when I went outside, she was on the ledge." His eyes begin to well with water and I've already put the puzzle together at this point.

"A nurse was on the roof trying to talk her down, but it didn't work. I watched my wife dive down to the pavement. At eighteen years old I was barely an adult but decided to do right by her and get married considering Eli was on the way. Even then, I never thought I'd see something like that. It made me grow up so fucking fast, but I guess shit does that to you."

"I am so sorry," I murmur, knowing there's nothing I can say. Even though I didn't know her I can't help but have tears welling behind my eyes. How he made it through that sort of tragedy . . . I have no idea.

"Thank you," His voice is quiet, and I didn't hear him. Thank goodness I can read lips most of the time. I turn around after the bass is getting so loud it's making the walls vibrate.

"Do you wanna go somewhere quiet so we can talk?" I ask, hollering, or at least trying to holler over the sound of the music.

Chaz nods his head and takes ahold of my hand as we weave in and out through the people, finally making it to the clubhouse door, he pushes it open and we get outside, where we can actually hear each other. "Give Izzy liquor and she becomes a DJ." Chaz chuckles, trying to lighten the mood.

"She's one of those women with many talents and whatnot," I laugh, getting a smile in response from him. He tugs slightly on my hand and I realize they're still interlaced. I pull his hand closer to the light and see the scars closer up. They must've healed well because you can't see much unless you're looking for them. Only a few of them are a bright pink, while most look like the ink they use for white tattoos.

"I was on a run with the club and we got jumped. Fucker tied us up and hurt us all. Shattered my hands," Chaz fills in the details, moving them around so I can see both sides.

"I'm sorry if I'm being crass, I only just noticed."

"Hey, it's fine. Means my personality kept you distracted for this long." He chuckles.

"Yeah, you could say that." I mutter under my breath, looking at him and roll my eyes.

I catch his smirk. "It happened a couple years back. Was a long recovery, but I'm good as new."

"Thank you for telling me, about your wife, and your hands." I speak lowly, looking into his eyes. I've never been in this position, so I'm not exactly sure how to thank someone for trusting me.

"Not sure I need to be thanked for that, but no problem." He chuckles.

I tighten my grip on his hand and look at him, not

sure if I'm making a huge mistake or not. So, I take in a deep breath and speak before I change my mind. "I blindsided Mircea because I wanted to know how he hurt you . . . because I care about you and I wanted to fix it. I put what he did together quickly."

"I thought you didn't speak to Mircea." Chaz grits.

"I avoid it at all costs. He's a dick, but . . . this was different. He. I need to tell you something, Charles." When I say his real name, his eyes widen and he takes a step back. A natural instinct I suppose.

"What's going on? You've never called me by that."

"Mircea made a remark about selling your family's whereabouts out to the new boss in France. I . . . I made a deal so that wouldn't happen. Or, Sorin made the deal for me, so nothing would happen to you."

"The fuck are you talking about, Crina?" Chaz hisses, taking two steps closer to me until we're chest to chest. "The fuck did you do?"

"I . . . shoved my pride down a hole and will bite my tongue to keep . . . to keep your family safe. You've become important to me. I don't know how it happened, but it did, and I can't bear being the reason something happens to you." I murmur as tears slowly begin to spill from the corners of my eyes. "I think you can figure out the relationship I have with my father is strained at best. I disowned my family when I got hired at Crave . . . but Mircea said if I apologized and made peace with my father, he wouldn't do as he threatened. I was distraught with emotion, so Sorin made the promise for me . . . Sorin is the only person in my family who's ever respected me. He's my big brother, and I love him dearly for what he did . . . because he saw I cared for you and didn't want me to have to make another sacrifice."

Chaz pushes his hands against my sternum until my back is pressed against one of the trees. We're maybe thirty feet away from the door of the club and my heart races a mile a minute as I try to figure out what he's doing.

"Why would you do something like that for me, stupid girl?" He whispers, pressing his forehead against mine. His eyes stare down into mine and I see the way his irises start to expand as if he's unleashing the beast within him.

"I already told you why." I reply in a shaky voice.

Chaz grows closer, bringing his rugged lips against mine. He's nothing like I've experienced before. Most of the men I've fucked have been pretty boys. The type who use Chapstick and put product in their hair. Not Chaz. He is all man.

Grazing my hand up his torso, I press against his muscles and feel the defined abs and pecs he has, then push my tongue past his teeth and clash with his. He grunts, intensifying the kiss out of nowhere.

I breathe in and out quickly, pawing at his jeans until I've unzipped his pants and pull his raging hard cock out. Luckily, I'm in a long flowy skirt, so I hike it up and he yanks my panties down. Lining himself up at my entrance he forces himself inside me.

I tear my lips away from his and lean my head against the tree behind me, moaning at the sudden intrusion. He shoves himself deeper into my canal, stretching my walls wide at his size. My pussy feels like it's on fire, raging with a divine wildfire. Yet, it feels heavenly. "Chaz," I moan his name as I rake my hands against his shoulders.

He hoists me up with one hand while he thrashes his hips against me. Just like the first moment he entered me, he doesn't relent, moving quicker and quicker. Chaz is fucking me so hard I know I'll feel this for days afterward.

He drags his tongue from the bottom of my neck until he's at my ear, pulling my lobe between his teeth, he whispers. "I've wanted to bury myself in your saturated cunt for so long. Do you like it when I fuck you like this?"

With the arm he's using to hoist me up, he firmly rubs his thumb against my hardening clit. I begin thrashing against his body, feeling his cock pulsating inside me. "Chaz, fuck. If you keep doing this I'm going to cum."

"That's the point, *brat*." He chuckles in a sinister manner, picking up his speed on both accounts, fucking me furiously while his thumb is greedily demanding me to release. "Motherfucker!" He hisses, stilling inside me. "Yes, that's it. You're so fucking close. I can feel your pussy begging for my cum."

"Y-yes, p-please." I bring a hand over my mouth and he rips it away.

"Fuck no. If I make you scream, you're going to fucking scream. No one will hear you anyway." Looking into his eyes, I've never seen such an evil glimmer before.

Chaz picks up his pace, ramming his cock into me so hard it sounds like he's fucking water. His balls slap against my lips and I feel the fly away saturation hit my legs and ass. "Fuck yes, fuck yes!" I belt out, feeling the euphoria take over until it feels like I'm floating.

"Yes, Crina. Fuck yes!" He snarls, finding his own release. He comes closer to me as we both orgasm, rocking his cock in and out of me slower, dragging both of our orgasms out.

Chaz takes me by the throat and looks directly into my eyes, "You fucking drive me crazy and I'm not letting you go. You're mine now. You understand that. Don't you?"

I'm sure this should've been a harder decision to make, but it isn't. I nod my head, confirming what he's just asked of me, knowing I did what will make me the happiest.

AUTHOR'S NOTE

Hey Guys,

So, that ended abruptly, right? Yeah, I know it did. I was writing and writing away at this story and just couldn't stop what I was doing. I didn't want to rush the progression between Chaz and Crina, but slowly show you how their connection begins to grow. One thing I also wanted to note is how I have plans . . . and these plans include giving you four points of view in Frost.

Yes, I said four.

No, I'm not fucking with you.

AUTHOR'S NOTE

While Frost is obviously Frost's story, Cheyenne is an integral part of it. It goes without being said that Chaz is a huge part of Cheyenne's life, and since I feel like I didn't finish writing about Chaz and Crina, I'm going to alternate between Frost, Cheyenne, Crina, and Chaz.

Rest assured, you will get your answers.

Xoxo,

Liz

Coming Soon: Demise

Want to find out what happens to Mircea? He's in Demise!

Pre-Order Here:

Coming Soon: Frost

Pre-Order Here:

Coming Soon: Corrupted Love

Pre-Order Here:

Coming Soon: Bossed Up

Pre-Order Here:

Coming Soon: Zorro

Pre-Order Here

Coming in 2021: Twisted Steel Second Edition

Pre-Order Here

Coming in 2021: The Elites

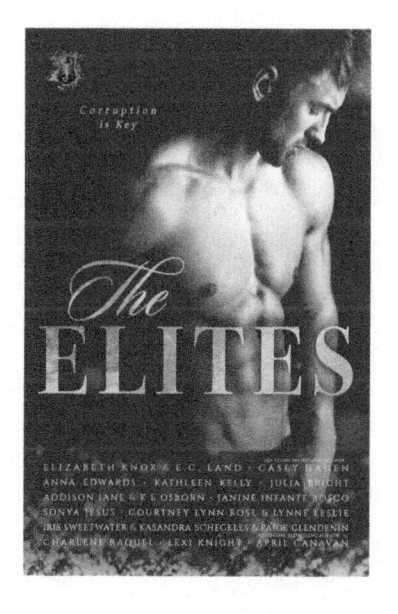

Get it Here

Made in United States
Orlando, FL
07 July 2024